MW00939108

# NIGHTINGALE

## ELLIE RAINE

PRO SE PRESS™

**PRO SE ⚑ PRESS**

NIGHTINGALE
A Pro Se Productions Publication

Written by Ellie Raine
Editing by Sean Taylor, Anna Munger

Cover by Antonino Lo Iacono
Book Design by Antonino Lo Iacono & Marzia Marina
New Pulp Logo Design by Sean E. Ali
New Pulp Seal Design by Cari Reese

www.prose-press.com

# CONTENTS

# PART I

# 1

His bloody tooth went flying when my pistol cracked his jaw, the molar clattering to the cement, quickly lost in the shadow of the alley. He spat blood, breathed a few heavy gasps and gritted his suddenly less-than-full set of choppers. "Fucker."

I shoved my .38 revolver against his head, digging the metal into his skull. "Try for that gun again, and I'll cover the brick with your daydreams."

"We had a deal."

"Still do."

It sounded like he muttered a curse, but the blood dribbling from his mouth made it too jumbled for me to make out. Then he spat out a dark glob at my feet and said, "I snooped around for that gal you asked after, but the deeper I dug, the more I found out about little-old you. You never said you're with the coppers."

"And I never said I wouldn't give you a new lead tooth either, but I will if you don't start talking, Darryl." I slapped the black-and-white photo of a light haired woman on the wall by his head, the picture brightened by the only light spilling into our alley from the nearby streetlamp. "You said you saw her," I kept my voice low. "You saw *this woman* here in Boston. Where? When? *Spill it.*"

Darryl cringed when I cocked the gun, and he

squealed. "All right, all right! Look, I don't know why you care, anyway. The dame didn't look important or nothing—"

"*Where?*"

"The opera house. Last night. She was poking around the back doors after hours."

"Was she with anyone?"

"Alone, I think. At least at first. I tailed her, though, and she met up with someone at a motel."

"Which one?"

Darryl licked his lips, but as he opened his mouth, a shot went off from the shadowed part of our alley and his brains painted the wall. He dropped as more shots blasted from the darkness and I grunted hard when one grazed my shoulder, a second hitting the dumpster beside me, and a third took out the streetlamp, shrouding the light along with it.

Stumbling in the new blackness and hearing another shot ring out behind me, I hurtled out to the curb and hung a left around the corner into the next alley over.

I waited, panting, clutching my burning shoulder and listened.

The shooting had stopped, and it was silent again. Cautious, I peeked around the corner. The dead man was still where I left him, but there was no sign of the shooter.

I was just about to creep back to take down the asshole who'd shot him, if anyone was still there, but the clicking sound of high heels echoed from down the street and glued my feet to the pavement. I stayed hidden, but inched my face around the wall with my pistol at my cheek.

I had to squint in the dark to see the approaching woman, but it wasn't until she passed under a farther, still lit streetlamp that I could make out her features. She was a tall gal aptly dressed for a funeral, hauntingly pale with bobbed raven-black hair that framed her sharp cheeks. A smoking stick was clamped between her teeth as she stepped toward the dead man at the alley's mouth.

The woman in black stopped when she reached the body. She took a good look at Darryl, unaware I was watching her. I saw her head cock at the corpse, and when she peered into the alley where the shots had come from, her square shoulders drooped.

"Well, well," she muttered, her feet shifting to a wider stance, as if getting ready to take on whoever stood in the darkness. "To what do I owe the pleasure?"

She trailed off, eyes suddenly darting to me. She had a cooling stare, the air feeling twice as cold. Even with my heavy coat, I had a mind to shiver, my breath fogging in front of me—

A loud croak blurted behind and I jumped, spinning. My breath caught. There was a crow perched on a rusty trash can. Its head twitched left and right, but its beady eyes stayed fixed on me. It opened its crooked beak and cawed at my face, lifting its wings and scraped its boney talons over the trash lid as it took a step closer.

I shuffled back. What the hell was a crow doing so close to the harbor? We usually saw seagulls.

The creepy bird stared at me for another few seconds, then croaked again and flew over my head.

I ducked and watched it glide down the sidewalk, landing beside the tall woman's heels.

She was still watching me, expression unchanged. Then she grinned and bent down, stroking the crow as gentle as if coddling a newborn baby. But her eyes stuck on me. It felt like she was examining the bones beneath my skin, studying the blood in the highway of veins in my muscles.

I expected her to call me out for snooping, but the broad only turned to look in the alley, and I barely heard her whisper a curse. Then she knelt between the crow and Darryl's corpse. It was like she didn't even notice the blood on the curb or the fact one side of his head was blasted open and missing some chunks when she touched his back. And then something else happened.

I wasn't sure my eyes were working right, but it looked like a faint, white mist was evaporating out of him, like meat cooking on a pan with simmering steam. When the mist disappeared, she rose and stole a last glance back at me. Then she walked back the way she'd come, the click of her heels fading with her.

"Hey," I called, walking up and keeping my revolver on hand while flattening my back against the wall at the mouth of the alley. Just because she wasn't pelted with lead already didn't mean the shooter was gone. "Stop! You're a witness to…"

She didn't even pause, and turned the corner at the next streetlight. I gritted my teeth, looking from Darryl to the place she'd left. As much as I wanted to run after her for questioning, leaving Darryl on the street seemed pretty damn irresponsible. Not to mention, his killer might still be near.

I winced when my shoulder flared with a faint pain. I'd been so distracted, I almost forgot I was grazed by a bullet earlier. Thankfully though, the sting was starting to fade. Quick healing really helped in my line of work. And speaking of work…

I got out a flashlight from my coat pocket, holding it up with my gun and then shined the beam of light over the dark alley. No one was there. Whoever killed Darryl was gone, in spite of my concerns.

"Damn it." I holstered my gun and shined the light on Darryl's body. I covered my nose with a sleeve to dampen the smell, gagging at the close-up of his blown head.

I hovered a hand over his back, checking for any more bullet holes. It looked like the headshot was the only hit. But what did that pale gal do to him? She must have put something on him to make that mist-looking stuff. Or had I imagined it?

"Damn it," I said again, rising to head for the telephone booth across the street. I originally wasn't going to involve the police, but a man was dead for God's sake. Captain Earl would have my head if I didn't fill him in.

I phoned the station, gave them a location, and after keeping watch of Darryl's body for half an hour and burning a Lucky Strike, I heard the quiet scream of sirens whining from uptown.

I was leaning against the brick wall when red and blue lights flashed from around the corner, and I flicked down my smoke and snuffed it with my shoe after the black and white sedans rolled up.

Officers started coming out and slamming doors, and I pushed off the wall to wave over one man in particular.

The heavy-waisted man saw me and headed my way, calling out. "Where's the stiff, Al?"

"This way," I told this district's police captain. "Watch the glass on the curb. The shooter took out the light."

He got out a flashlight and swept the beam over the sidewalk to see the glinting shards and took care to step around them. Captain Earl Hunter was a towering man, almost too tall to fit under standard-sized doorways. He was round in the middle with wide shoulders and a thick neck. His brown overcoat fell to his knees, belt cinched tight at his waist where a .22 Magnum was tucked snuggly.

Earl and I went way back, from the early days when I first joined the force. He and I were still basic officers then; we got along throughout the years. Some time after he was promoted to lieutenant and I joined the CID, I decided to leave and work for myself, for personal reasons. Earl understood. I had someone to find. And I realized down the road that I wouldn't find her using the department's methods.

I still had some pull with the cops thanks to Earl, and he often came to my office for consultation on cases. And ever since he was promoted to captain, I'd found myself in a pretty comfortable financial situation, what with the consistent work from him and other private clients. It wasn't where the big bucks were, but it paid the bills well enough and put food on the table.

Earl bent next to Darryl and aimed the flashlight up and down. "One shot at the head, another at the light." He shined the light at the dumpster and brick wall behind me. "Two in the bricks and one on the trash. Were any more bullets let loose, or is that it?"

"I think one went out to the street," I said, squinting and raising a hand to my eyes when he shone the beam at my face.

"Christ, Al, looks like one got you." He sounded alarmed now, rising to get a closer look at my shoulder.

"Oh, yeah. Forgot about that." The pain had disappeared completely now, so I hadn't given it anymore thought. The sleeve was soaked red around the open tear, still wet and sticky.

Earl hollered at the medics who came with them. "Hey, someone get over here and take this guy to the hosp—!"

"No," I interrupted. "No hospital. It, er... wasn't a bullet. There was wet paint near my apartment and I wasn't paying attention."

He stared so intently at my sleeve, one of his eyes looked ready to pop a blood vessel. "And the tear?"

"It snagged on a nail in the phone booth."

"Snagged on a nail my ass." He grabbed my arm and pried open the tear. "I know blood when I damn well see it."

The breath fell out of him when he saw my bare shoulder. It was perfectly smooth and unscathed, not a scar to be seen, despite all the blood.

He looked from the shoulder to my face. "It... sure looks like blood..."

"Does, doesn't it?" I shrugged out of his grasp, taking out a pack of Lucky's from my coat pocket and lit one up. "But it's paint."

"Paint…" he looked back at the shoulder. "I know you said you were a fast healer once, but…"

I lifted an eyebrow. "If it was blood, I think I'd have a pretty ugly gash, yeah? No one heals that quick." No one except my brother and me, as far as I knew. But Earl didn't need to know that.

Seeming to buy it, he nodded and scratched his balding head. "Damn convincing paint." he shined his light back on Darryl, focusing back on task. "So, who's the stiff?"

"Darryl Heler," I said. "I was getting info from him before someone decided to use him for target practice."

He squatted down and started patting Darryl's pockets, finding a wallet, some keys, and a crushed pack of Marlboros. He rifled through the wallet. "Were you getting info for a client?"

"Personal reasons."

His gaze flicked up at me. "Henrietta?"

"Henrietta," I confirmed. "Turns out she's here in Boston."

"Jesus." He stretched to his feet and handed Darryl's belongings to a man from Police Science and Criminalistics, who bagged it and ran it over to his team. Earl turned back to me. "Think the shooting's involved with your search?"

"I'd be a pretty damn terrible investigator if I didn't think so. It's too convenient. Practically every informant I get something out of gets terminated one way or another. And this is the first time I hear she's in town, so I'd be willing to bet she's the shooter herself."

He nodded, grunting. "Did you find out a specific location?"

"Darryl only saw her snooping around the opera. That's all I got before he bit the bullet."

"I'll send some boys to stake the place out. Come on, I'll give you a ride home. I don't want you walking out here with a shooter on the loose."

"Right. Just my office will do. I have to file all this mess."

He nodded, and I followed him to his car, watching from the passenger window as the boys bagged Darryl's body and loaded him in the ambulance that came with the black-and-white cavalry.

Earl shouted some orders at the officers and slid inside behind the wheel, starting the ignition. He drove us off the street and further into the busier side of town, hanging a left on Franklin street. Other cars screeched their tires when they hit the brakes, horns blared left and right, and people walked across the street whenever they felt like. It took twenty minutes in that traffic before we reached my office, and when I opened the door and stepped out, I paused and glared back inside the car at Earl.

"You're not going to keep me in the dark on a single speck of dust in this case, you get me?" I said. "You find even a strand of hair you think belongs to her, you call me. I'll be damned if this rug is pulled out from under me by the cops."

He grinned and folded his arms over the wheel.

"You're already involved, son. You're a witness, *and* a consultant. Whether you like it or not, if we find anything, you'll be the first guy I call."

"Damn right I will be."

I shut the door and watched him drive off, fishing for my keys. My office was on the first floor. It was a small space wedged between an old consignment shop and a launderer. Nothing fancy, but that was how I liked it.

I walked up to my door, the glass window reading *Alastor Déus, P.I.* in bold, black letters, with the *s* peeling off. I tried to rub the dried paint back on the glass with a finger, shivering. It was getting colder, little by little tonight. Something felt off. The traffic in the street was still as loud as ever, late night prowlers drunkenly stumbling and laughing outside the bar across the street, but the noise sounded dampened. It was like my ears were underwater.

I let out a foggy breath and slid the key in the lock…

Croaking caws blurted behind me and I damn near jumped out of my skin. Across the street, I saw a group of crows huddled on the ground eating a mangled seagull carcass. Kneeling by the flock was a black-haired woman, the same pale broad from the crime scene, petting the crows and staring at me across the traffic.

It only took me a shocked moment to get my legs moving and I headed to her, but I leapt back when a van pulled up in front of me and laid on the horn. I went around and kept on track, but had to stop again for another car, and then another.

Stuck where I was, I saw the woman rise to her feet and start down the road and around the block. There was finally an opening in the street and I rushed after her, but caught sight of her getting into a cab before it drove off.

After it sped away, I kicked a newsstand, startling the surrounding crows as they screeched and flew off. Damn that creepy broad and those dirty, winged rats. Was she keeping tabs on me?

Remembering I left the key in the lock, I clicked my tongue and went back across the street. Fine. Let her poke around. At least she knew where I worked. If she was here once, chances were, she'd be back. It would just give me more opportunity to catch her for questioning. And boy was she in for one hell of an interrogation.

# 2

The cab pulled into the driveway, dirt and pavement crunching under the tires as the breaks squeaked to a stop.

Grabbing my three bags of groceries, I hefted myself out of that car and breathed in the morning air. Last night had been a living hell, and the search for Henrietta has never been this close. I was itching to get out there and keep to it, but I had to put it aside for today. Not only did my sister-in-law need food for the week, but my brother was supposed to come back from the war. He got an early discharge, according to the letter his wife got in the mail a couple months ago. It said he was injured, lost his whole damn leg to a Nazi landmine. It was a relief he was alive, at least, and being sent home. His wife, Sun, was going to make a damn good lunch for him. Like hell I was going to miss that.

His family had a quaint little home in the outskirts of town. It was a small house, like the ones you'd see in the papers, the kind that seemed a little too wholesome to be real with its white exterior and happy red shutters. It seemed a little cramped for a family of four, but these days, my brother's wife and kids were used to minimal luxuries. They counted their blessings that they still *had* a house.

When the cabbie drove off, I walked down the

stone path, but stopped short when I found a woman planting a small patch of tiger lilies by the door. Her face was hidden under a wide-rimmed, wicker hat, with a scarf that was wrapped all around her head.

"Sun," I said sternly, walking to my sister-in-law and looking around to make sure no one else was here. "If you want flowers, you should let me do it. You can't be out here."

"I can be wherever I damn well want in my own yard." She dug her spade into the dirt and wiped her gloves on her skirt, looking up at me with black, angled eyes under the hat. "I just found these growing behind the house and thought Ollie would like to see some color in the front when he comes home."

"You know what else he'd like to see? His family still at home and not taken to an internment camp for being Japs. Now go on, I got what you asked for at the market. Need help with the cooking?"

She sighed, standing to get the door. "No, I'll handle it. Thanks, Al. But you could help set the table."

"Sure could." I followed her in, kicking the door closed behind me and followed her to the kitchen, setting the groceries on the counter.

Sun got to cooking while I got out the plates and silverware, and when I went to get the glasses, my five year old niece came barreling in, latching to my waist.

"Uncle Al!" The chubby brunette tightened her grip, crushing me. "You were s'pose to come hours ago!"

"Five minutes isn't exactly a few hours, Stephanie." I chuckled and ruffled her hair, grinning at her black, almond-shaped eyes. "But it's nice to see you too, sweetheart."

Sun lit up the stove and poured some oil on the pan, getting a deeper pot up there next and started boiling water.

I pried off Stephanie. "Why don't you get your brother? Tell him he'd better get his rear out of bed if he wants any of this fine dining."

She gave a toothy grin and hurried out while I got the glasses from the cupboard and set them on the table. Sun began humming a jig as she chopped up two tomatoes at the counter, bobbing her head to her own beat. She'd taken off her scarf and hat, letting her black hair fall to her shoulders.

Sun had a young face for a woman nearing 40. Hell, I'd been mistaken for 35, almost being 50, but that was my Greek blood. We looked young. I guessed the Japs had the same perk.

Stephanie came back soon enough, dragging her older brother behind her. Stephanie's real name was Cephísso. It was Greek—my brother loved our heritage—but most Americans here couldn't pronounce it right. So, to keep things simple, her parents picked an easier-to-say nickname.

My fourteen-year-old nephew didn't look happy to be up, his black hair tussled and lids baggy with morning grogginess, but when he saw me, his expression relaxed.

"Hey, Uncle Al," he yawned when opening the refrigerator to take the pitcher of lemonade. He poured himself a drink, put back the pitcher and slumped into a seat at the table, rubbing his eyes.

"Morning, Syrus," I slid into the chair across from him. "Up late, eh?"

Syrus shrugged and took a few glugs of his juice. His mother piped up while slicing an onion. "He was studying. I'm giving him an exam next week, in science. His last score was less than great, so I'm giving him another try."

"Ah," I grinned at Syrus. "Well, good to see you're studying in the wee hours of the morning for it," I gave him a sharp look.

He propped an elbow on the table to hold up his head, grunting. But he perked when a car door slammed outside. Not long after, the door squeaked open.

"Anyone home?" called my brother's well missed voice from the front.

We all got up, Sun abandoning the stove as we went for the door. I had no idea what I would see, after he'd been gone for over a year. The letter said his leg had been blown off. I guess that meant he'd be in a wheelchair for the rest of his life. He'd need help getting around…

I paused when I saw him, everyone else pushing ahead of me.

There he was, my brother Ollie, taking off his brown leather boots and throwing off the duffle bag around his shoulder when Stephanie latched onto his leg—of which he had both.

Ollie picked up Stephanie in a chuckle, slinging the girl over his shoulder. "Cephísso, *Mikró Louloúdi*. Just look at how big you've gotten."

He kissed her cheek and turned to the opened

door, waving outside at the cabbie that'd dropped him off, signaling that he didn't need it to stay. The car rolled off as he shut the door with his intact foot, setting Stephanie down to hug his son next. Syrus breathed out a "Welcome home, dad" before Ollie went to take his wife by the waist.

"*Ilios mou,*" he greeted with a kiss. That was 'my sun' in Greek. Years of practically being raised by my older brother had made me bilingual. Not that anyone here in Boston cared, and neither did anyone understand us. We only threw out the foreign talk around family.

Sun was also fluent. They'd met in Greece, before I came around, though I was never sure how long ago it was. They kept changing the number when I asked.

When Ollie let her go, he smiled at me and clasped my hand before giving me a strong hug. "Al, good to see you."

"Same to you," I said, hesitating. "Glad to see you're still in… one piece. The letter we got said your leg was blown off."

His smile staled. There was something about his eyes that didn't seem right. They looked guarded. Or maybe haunted? "They must have meant my buddy Eddy. He was in my platoon, and… well…" He sniffed and scratched a finger under his army cap. "Uh, so, how's work been? It's been a while, hope Earl's still giving you enough cases."

"Oh, I get plenty." I guessed he was done talking about the war. Probably better if I dropped it. "And this latest case takes the cake."

He looked curious. "What is it?"

"I'll, uh, tell you about it over drinks later." I pushed the kids back toward the kitchen. "Wouldn't want Sun's fine cooking to get cold."

Ollie and Sun followed behind, and I heard Sun whisper to him. "So? Any luck finding…?"

I glanced back to see Ollie shake his head and take off his cap, showing his cropped brown hair. Then he slid out a cigarette and lit it between his lips.

Sun sighed, taking a brief second to brood on whatever that had meant. But when she caught my eye, she put on a new smile and her voice rose to a more chipper tune. "Oh, I think the water's boiling."

She hurried to the stove as we all went to the table, pouring the pasta sticks into the pot.

***

After lunch, I took Ollie into town, to relax and get a feel for city life again. We went to see a flick, then that evening I took him to a bar two blocks away from the theater.

We sat at the counter and listened to the band in the back, and I waited until we both had our drinks before clearing my throat. "So. There's news on my hunt."

He took a sip from his glass and raised an eyebrow at me. "With Henrietta? Christ Almighty, Al, haven't I told you to drop it? She's not someone you want to find."

"Well, don't have much choice now, do I?"

He eyed me narrowly. "What are you yapping

about?"

"Something tells me you aren't going to like the tip I got last night."

"And what poor schmuck gave you that tip? Better question," he said and turned so he could look me straight in the eye. "Is that poor schmuck still alive?"

My shrug was half-hearted. "It's not my fault someone keeps scratching off my leads."

"Actually, it is." His glass clipped the counter. "You know better. You know what Ma's capable of."

I did. Not that I knew much better than Ollie, since I was only six last time I saw her. But it was a time I'd never forget.

Ollie smeared a hand over his face. "Al, look. Do me a favor. Stop looking for that old hag. What do you even expect to do if you find her?"

"The same thing she did to Pop," I said. "I'm going to put a bullet through her teeth."

That was the most distinct memory I had of my childhood up in New York. Everything before that point was pretty blurry, but the deafening *bang* of her gun going off in Pop's mouth, the dark splatter on the wallpaper behind him, the back of his skull exploding onto the window shades in the kitchen, Pops falling over like a sack of meat...

Ollie had grabbed me and skedaddled out of there, but it'd been two seconds too late. I'd seen everything. And I never forgot.

He ran a hand through his short hair, the bags under his lids dark and puffy. For a second there, he actually looked years older. But damn him, he still didn't look a day over 25. And he was the older brother. Greek blood aside, even *I* couldn't pull that off. Damned lucky bastard.

He shot me a sidelong look, amber eyes glinting like sunbeams in the dim light, and took a swig of his scotch. "And after that?" he asked, voice coarse and low. "After you shoot her, what's next on your to-do list?"

I shrugged. "Won't know till I get there."

He sighed, seeming to give up. After another glug, he said. "So, what was the tip? If your informant died over it, it'd better have been worth it."

"It was." My smile was wicked. "Better have Sun cook up a nice dinner. Looks like the family reunion's come to us."

He almost choked on his drink. "God, no. Don't say it."

"She's in Boston," I said, nodding to the front door, where the opera house waited just around the corner. "At the theater, to be specific."

"Damn it." He dropped his head, trying to shield his face with a hand. "God fucking damn it. When?"

"A few nights back."

"What the hell is she…" he was muttering more to himself than to me now, staring hard at the counter. Then he blinked. "Wait. What year is it again? '43?"

"'44," I corrected, guessing the months at war had done a number on his sense of time.

His fingers started twitching, as if counting down. "Shit. It's been that long?"

"What, since we've seen Ma?" I took a long swig of my drink, spilling some on my tie and cursing while wiping a napkin over it. "Guess so. Forty-two years of being a ghost and now she just pops up? And I don't even have to hop a few states—or even a few countries—for it? Damn crazy luck for me, that's for sure."

"It isn't luck," he growled, clutching his glass. "She's here for a reason."

The stain wouldn't come out of my tie, and I loosened it to take it off my neck. Not having anywhere else to put it, I rolled it into a pocket. "What reason do you think she's here for?"

"Just—" he was interrupted when the band's music burst with a loud note from the trumpet, and a few slaps of the symbols and jazzy trombones blurted. Only when the swelling went back to its quieter volume did he continue in a mutter. "Call it a hunch."

I kept to my drink, careful not to spill it this time. "Oh. There was something else."

He *thunked* his elbows on the counter and rubbed his eyes. "Don't say that. Her being here is bad enough."

"There was another dame there last night, when my guy was shot."

He groaned. "Well, isn't that just swell. Who else?"

"Don't know her name. She was a spooky looking gal. Pale as a ghost. Seems to have a thing for disgusting scavenger birds. And I think…" I took out a Lucky and lit it up, puffed, then let out a smooth, smoky stream. "I think she did something

21

to my informant's body. I don't know what, though. It was dark, but it kind of looked like…" I glugged the rest of my glass, then clacked it down on the counter. "Never mind. I was probably seeing things."

"Yeah," he muttered, finishing his own drink and staring into the empty cup. "I'd say you're right, there."

"Come on," I nodded to the door and got up, putting cash on the table to pay for the drinks, then swiped my hat off the counter. "Want to do some snooping around with me at the theater?"

"Hell no. Go and take a look yourself if you want, but I have to warn Sun and the kids. I swear to god, if Henrietta shows up…"

He rose from his stool, then went to hail a cab. It was dark out now, the few city lights speckling the streets and cluttered buildings. I waited till Ollie was on his way home before starting down the street toward the opera house alone.

Well, so much for the extra help. But at least he knew about it, and the others would know to lay low. Probably best that he went to warn them. No telling what Ma might do if she found them.

*But she's not going to have the chance.* Tipping down my hat, I had my fingers brush the pistol at my hip. *I'll blast a hole in her windpipe before she can tell them howdy-do.*

I sped up the pace toward the opera house.

"You might not want to go that way."

I twisted at the voice, scanning the mildly busy street, but didn't see any faces looking my way. Then the same voice purred to my left. "Right here, big cat."

My head shot in that direction, and it didn't take me long to find her. Sitting at a café's outdoor table and smoking from a long stick right next to me was a dark haired broad in a black, wide-rimmed hat. It was the same woman from last night. She wasn't looking at me, but reading from the papers with an empty cup of Joe on the table. I staggered, blinking to make damn sure I was seeing straight.

Yep. I was.

"Well, this must be my lucky day." I leaned over and slammed a hand on the table. "Listen here, doll. You and me are going to have a little talk. And I don't expect to do much of it, get me?"

Her ruby lips drew in a soft breath through her smoking stick before breathing it out in a smooth wisp of grey. "Sounds great, big cat," she said and set down the paper to look at me, her long gams crossing. The stick waved in circles and left hypnotic smoke trails between us. "But I don't expect to start wagging my tongue till you give me answers *I* want."

I narrowed my lids. "Not how it works."

She got up and walked the way I was originally headed, beckoning me with a wave of her stick. "Mind if we walk and talk? I'm in a hurry."

"To the opera?" I fell into step behind her with a cautious gait. "I take it you got someone to meet there? A trigger-happy buddy, maybe?"

Her black glare was sharp. But mine was sharper.

Now that I was this close to her, she didn't seem as spooky as I remembered. She looked like any other young gal you'd find in the city—if every other gal's regular hangout was a funeral home. Except for her vivid lipstick, the only other speck of color on her was a brilliant, red gem embedded into the ornate centerpiece of her smoking stick, and two garnet earrings. But the latter looked dull in comparison. That first stone seemed to glitter with its own light. Trick of the gem's cut, I guessed.

Her scrutiny ended with a smoky hum. "If you think she and I are 'buddies,' then I guess you don't know much about us after all. That's one question off my list."

She was about to strut off, but I grabbed her shoulder. "She? You talking about Darryl's killer?"

"If Darryl was your friend who was swimming in his own brain-pool last night, then yeah. Sure."

"So, a dame did him in?" I gave a toothy grin. "Then, my money's definitely on her. Henrietta hasn't given up her old habits, it looks like."

She squinted an eye. "You know Henrietta?"

"You could say we're acquainted."

Her heels circled the cement until she faced me front and center, and she crossed her arms. One set of manicured fingernails drummed on her arm while the other raised the smoking stick to her lips.

"What?" I asked.

"You look like him." Smoke puffed with the last syllable. "Too much like him."

"Like who, doll. The game is twenty questions, not riddles and rhymes."

She didn't answer. Instead, she asked. "What's your name, big cat?"

"Alastor Déus." I pulled out my business card

from my coat pocket. "Private Investigator. And you're on the wrong end of this investigation, toots, so now I'm asking for your name."

She sucked in a breath, looking ripe to answer, but stopped herself. Her clipped tone let me know this was the response she was sticking with. "Dee."

"Got a last name with that, Dee?"

She threw up a blithe hand and spun forward, heading on the path again. "I'll let you figure that one out, Mr. Investigator."

I followed behind her. "All right, forget the name. But let's get something straight, sugar." I took my pistol from its holster and dug the barrel into her back, keeping it close to my stomach to hide it from the other pedestrians. "I got a list of questions the size of Virginia that I want to know. And it sounds like you know more about what's going down at the opera. So move it. And don't even think about putting those pretty heels to work in the wrong direction."

She didn't move, but sounded confused. "A gun? Why bother?"

"I like the security."

"What security?" She was stifling a laugh, as if this was some playful joke.

"Of knowing *I* have the pistol, and *I'm* the one who can blow your guts to oblivion, and not the other way around. Now shut your trap before I shut it for you."

Her laughter died. She craned back to look at me like I was crazy. Then she turned forward again and huffed. "Well. That's one more question off my list. Anyway, may as well tuck it, tiger. That little toy of yours is as threatening as a cap gun. But dinner might get you pretty far, if you make it a nice one."

"How about we save dinner for the next date? I'm feeling like a show tonight."

She sighed and started walking as I kept a close pace behind her.

I kept to my armed interrogation. "How do you know Henrietta? Is she your partner? A friend? A..." This one felt weird to ask. "A relative?"

She spat out a laugh. "Good god, if I was one of her kids, I think I'd *really* want to kill myself."

I frowned. There was something creepy with that phrasing. "You've wanted to kill yourself before?"

She shrugged, as if I'd asked her something as mundane as her morning laundry routine. "We've all thought about it."

"I know plenty of people who, I'm pretty sure, have not."

"I'm not talking about everyone in the world, big cat. I'm talking about me and the others."

"Are you in some kind of cult?"

"I wouldn't call it a cult, but whatever helps you sleep at night," she paused, looking back at me again. "You do sleep, don't you?"

"Who in hell doesn't sleep?"

"We used to have someone who didn't. But he clocked out a while back, and sometimes new recruits get similar traits as the old ones. You just never know these days."

"What in hell are you..."

I staggered when noticing the road blocks and

swarm of cops at the front of the opera. I knew Earl said he'd send a few of the boys out to search the place, but I didn't think he'd take it this far. Did something happen?

I told Dee to walk faster, putting my gun away before grabbing her arm to make sure she didn't make a run for it. We got close to the main attraction just as a copper ran up to stop us. But he shut his yapper when he got close enough to see my face.

"Oh," stammered the officer. "Mr. Déus. The captain was looking for…" He eyed Dee with no subtle glance, his peepers working their way up her gams. He cleared his throat and redirected. "Who's this?"

"My… secretary." My grip tightened on her arm as I shoved past him, hustling to the heart of the swarm. Earl was here himself? Jesus, it had to be serious.

I found Earl waiting for me outside the front steps. A shapely fedora covered his messy black hair, and he alternated between taking the hat off and putting it on. He was also scratching his chin raw, something he usually did when things were bad.

When he saw me heading his way, he jabbed a fat finger at me, then threw a thumb over his shoulder at the opera house. That was his way of saying 'follow me and don't say a damn word until we're inside.' I knew better than to argue, so Dee and I trailed him when he shoved through the revolving doors.

The opera itself was an impressive sight, no

matter what angle you were looking from. I'd only been here a couple times with a few lady friends, but the lobby seemed… emptier tonight, excluding the coppers crawling all over the place. Most of the employees were absent, the concessions abandoned, ushers and clerks downright AWOL. There should have been a crowd, given the advertising signs saying an orchestra was scheduled to play half an hour ago, but there were no spectators here. The left behind wine glasses—half filled—on the tables meant there *had* been people, but I guessed the chief had everyone evacuated for… whatever the hell was going on.

Midway through the lobby, Earl's wingtips squeaked to a halt, and he whirled on me. "Where the hell have you been?" he snapped, face red and belligerent. "I called you hours ago!"

I shrugged, discreetly letting Dee go when I was sure she'd stay put. "I was out with my brother," I explained. "He just got back from the war."

"Great to hear," he spat, though I knew he sincerely meant it. The gravity of this situation just outweighed it, so it came out as dark sarcasm. His eyes flicked to Dee. "This isn't a date, Al, get her the hell out of here."

"She stays," I said. "New secretary."

"Since when did you start looking for a secretary?"

"Thought it was overdue."

He grunted, taking off his hat to rub his balding head. "Guess you never do answer your damn phone."

"Exactly. And I need her to take, er… notes.

She stays."

Earl shook his head. "Fine. But don't blame me if she skedaddles after this... Tighten your stomach, Al. It ain't pretty. I've never seen something like this, and frankly, I don't know how to handle it just yet."

"Stop squawking and show me already."

He nodded and led Dee and me to the performance room. Dee lit a new cigarette on her smoking stick and inhaled, sighing. "Hope you're ready, big cat."

I eyed her suspiciously. "Just shut your trap, doll, and don't even think of..."

As soon as the door opened, the stench hit my nostrils like pickled razors. Then I saw the display on stage.

Lord Almighty.

# 3

Camera flashes blinked onstage, capturing the main attraction that brought us all here. Her body was strung up by wires on a nearby chair, one hand placed on the cello's strings and the other limply gripping the long bow. She would have looked like any normal, poised musician about to play a masterpiece.

Except her detached head was speared to the cello's neck.

"What in the seven hells is this, Earl?" I demanded, both of us stepping up to the stage with green faces. "A damned pig roast?"

Earl could only shake his head and pinch his nose as we got closer to the human sculpture. "Why do you think I phoned you? I want to know what happened, why, when, and what deranged little fucker did it."

I cupped a hand over my own nose, getting as close as I dared to the marionette. I had to swat the flies away while prodding her hand with a pen. It wouldn't budge, the fingers strapped to the cello's strings. "Tied with steel wire, looks like. Why would—*huch...!*" I'd loosened my covering hand a fraction and was met with the god awful, sour stench of decay. I bent over and gagged, then hurriedly got out my kerchief to block my nose. The thin fabric didn't help much.

I swallowed vomit, got a hold of myself... then I noticed something new with the body. At this angle, I could see a giant hole had been carved in her chest cavity. "Oh, damn," I muttered. "Tell me her heart's where it should be?"

Earl seized the cello's neck and shook it lightly. A series of low *thunks* rapped from inside. I took out a penlight from my coat pocket and shined the beam through the instrument's hole. There it was: a soggy lump of heart-meat, extra pulverized.

"Christ almighty." I fastened the kerchief to my nose again, more than eager to look for extra details *elsewhere*.

The performance room grew quiet as I studied the scene. I caught the eyes of several criminologists looking both curious and sick, lingering in the front row like a bunch of vultures.

Dee had perched her pretty rear in a seat among them, her long legs crossed and kicking leisurely as she kept to her smoke. She was staring at the ceiling, where a few crows had found a way in and alighted on the overhanging rafters. Guess she was set on watching the show.

Focusing back, I felt along the cello's base, then trailed up the slick lacquer. If there were any scuff marks or dents, it might suggest a struggle, if the instrument was involved at all. Hell, it could have been the murder weapon for all I knew, before the lunatic chopped her up.

I stopped at the neck when my fingers brushed over an etching there, and I peered close. There were strange symbols written in the wood. They were crude and uneven, but at least legible.

Legible if you could read Greek. Which I could.

"*Thymitheíte Orféa*," I read aloud.

I was about to tell Earl the translation, but Dee spoke up first, still looking at the crows. "Remember Orpheus."

Something about her tone made me shudder. Putting aside the fact she knew Greek, it was eerie how she wouldn't take her eyes off the ceiling, staying in her seat with lax posture, the grey smoke curling from her stick. Her face was damn near unreadable. But I caught the subtle tremor in her fingers, making her cigarette holder shake and give away her nervousness.

After nearly a full minute of her voice going dead, I prodded from the stage. "Do you know what that means?"

Her stare flicked to the captain, then back to me. "No."

That was a lie. Her dark glare was telling me that loud and clear. Those words meant something to her. I wasn't sure what, but I knew I didn't like it. Whatever she knew, though, it looked like she wasn't willing to spill until we were away from the crowd. Fine by me.

Earl grumbled next to me. "Think it's some kind of statement?"

"Could be," I said. "Sounds like a fable reference, but I'll have to get more details. Who was the broad anyway?"

"Fairly famous cellist from New York. She was scheduled to perform tonight, but that obviously ain't happening. The director's in a fit over it."

"Can't blame him." I glanced at the red-faced

man causing a small ruckus in the back row of seats, chewing out some of the officers. He was dressed in a fancy tux and black bowtie, wiping the sweat from his receding hairline.

I gave a loud, echoing whistle, catching his attention. I waved for the man in the tux—whom I had a hunch was the house director—to come up, and I met him in the aisle halfway.

"Evening." I shook his hand. "You in charge here?"

"Y-yes." He wiped his brow with a kerchief. "Stephen Beckham, house director."

I gave him one of my business cards. "Alastor Déus. Private Investigator."

His brow screwed up, looking closer at the picture. "They're letting college kids snoop around for the press?"

"I'm 48, sir," I muttered. "I haven't been to school in a good twenty years."

His eyes popped open at me. Then he glanced over my shoulder—at Dee, who'd apparently followed me over here—and looked for confirmation. She gave him a nodding shrug, and Beckham shook his head. "Hot damn. They must be putting something in the water these days."

"No sir, just Greek blood." I reeled the topic back into focus. "So, Captain Hunter asked me to take a peek at your... problem."

Beckham's eyes flicked at the stage and he gagged, shoving the handkerchief to his nose. "I... Y-yes, thank you."

I took out a notepad and pen from my coat pocket, flipping to a clean page. "Now tell it to me straight. As much as you remember, from what you had for breakfast to now."

He told me everything. Most of it was useless, but I listened anyway, writing down notes. He said he didn't sleep last night because he was nervous for the cellist's opening night and stayed up smoking, killing a bottle of bourbon, talking with some people on the telephone, making sure everything was set for tonight, yadda, yadda...

Beckham was fidgeting with the kerchief when he swallowed next. "I was just about to leave the house when I got the call about Pammie—"

"The cellist?" I interjected, brow lifting. "Sorry, no one's told me her name yet."

"Ah, yes, it's... er, *was*... Pamela. Rutheford."

*Pet name basis,* I noted. That usually meant some relationship, which was hinted from the endearing tone he used. I stole a glance at the man's ring finger. Fitted with a gold band. Judging from his tear-free eyes—despite his sickly green complexion—I took it this broad wasn't his wife. Probably a lover. Not that it mattered. Maybe.

Saving that bit for later, I slipped out the old picture of Henrietta and showed it to the director. "Now, Mr. Beckham, did you happen to see this woman in or near the building recently?"

His face blanched. "Oh, hell. Is she dead, too?"

"Don't I wish," I muttered. "You recognize her?"

"I, uh..." He shifted his weight uncomfortably. "We, er... might have met for an 'appointment' once..."

I tried not to grimace. Failed. "When?"

"Er, sixteen—no." He paused to think. "Nineteen hours ago. Left the opera at one o'clock last night."

I sighed and smeared a hand over my mouth. "Was that before or after your 'appointment' with our *cellist* over there?"

The shock choked out of him. "I—well, I... Just what are you suggesting?"

"I'm an investigator, sir, don't insult me. Before or after?"

He squeaked a small, nervous laugh. "During..."

"Good god man, what's wrong with you? The dead brunette I can understand, but that old bat's got to be at least 70 by now."

"Boy if she was, then there's definitely something in the water. Looked exactly the way she is in the picture, not a hair out of place."

I looked at the picture again, raising an eyebrow. "This was taken over 40 years ago."

"Well, I tell you what," he laughed. "She must've found the secret, because those gams were moving like weasels—"

"Don't." Even my thoughts were groaning, and I raised a hand to beg him to shut the hell up. I sighed. "Was there anyone else in the House I should know about?"

His head shook.

I massaged my temples. "Right, well. Thank you for your time..."

The photo went back into my pocket as I stomped out of there, desperate to knock out that new mental image of the director's little affairs... I shuddered and shut it out.

"Mommy troubles?"

I jumped at the voice, whirling to see Dee had followed me out to the lobby. I forgot she was there. Before I growled at her to keep her trap shut, I paused.

"What makes you think she's my mother?" I assumed Dee saw the picture when I showed it to Beckham, but I never said who she was.

She only shrugged. "Who else could she be?"

"Just based on the photo? Anyone. But if you're in her little cult, then she must have mentioned she had a son at one of your meetings, huh?"

Her chuckle purred from her lips. "What other family have you met? Any brothers? Sisters? An uncle or two?"

My tone guarded. "My family's none of your damn business."

"Don't I wish, big cat," she sighed. "The problem is, you all keep dragging me back in the game every time I find a nice place to settle down for a while."

"What does that..." I glanced around, noticing some of the coppers bustling in the lobby had stopped to look at us. I pursed my lips and nodded towards the door. "Walk with me."

She complied without question or complaint, and after we cleared the revolving doors and headed down the noisy, horn-blaring block, I took out a pack of Luckys and lit one up.

"Talk." Smoke spilled from my nose with the order. "What did you mean by 'you all' and 'game?' And what the hell was that message on the cello about?"

"To answer your first question," she began musingly. "By 'you all' I meant the Déus family. I wasn't sure you were one of them until you flashed me your card."

I wasn't following. There were so many pieces missing, and it was like she forgot she needed to start from the top. I prodded. "What do you know about my family?"

"More than I'd like to." Her heels clicked over the cement. "To be honest, it's always one of you who starts the wars. Oh, sure, the others have their skirmishes every now and then, but they don't usually involve the rest of us. Only when a Déus is in the area does everyone have problems. Always trying to recruit us to their sides, extra cash and authority promised, *rarely* paid back, mind you, and not to mention—"

"What the hell are you saying?" I stopped her with a hand to the shoulder. "You make it sound like you're all part of the damn mafia."

"Something like that," she considered. "Got to be honest, it gets harder to care about all these laws the longer you go on. They're always changing anyway, and what do we have to worry about except being stuck in some boring cell block for a while? Not much incentive to follow the rules when you take away the most important fear known to man."

"What fear?"

"Death." She shrugged.

I stared at her. "You don't fear death?"

"It's not that we don't fear it." She shifted her

weight and waved her stick around, making smoky circles next to her head. "Hell, there've been some of us who've pined for it, the sad sacks... No, we just don't worry about it anymore. Not unless it's the right time."

I made a low, sarcastic laugh. "Like when there's a gun to your head?"

She grinned. "Not quite."

"Right... well, doll." I sucked on the Lucky, breathing out the spice. "You say you know some of my family. Which is how you know about my mother. And if you say some of them are in crime gangs, you'll know if *she's* in one."

"In one?" It was her turn to laugh. "Daddy-O, your old lady *is* one. She runs a whore house up north."

Fuck. I pinched my nose and sighed. "Great. Then what is she doing here if her gig's up north?"

"Based on the beautiful display at the opera?" She threw her head back. "She's here for the stash."

"What stash? Like money?"

She tapped her smoking stick with a finger, flicking off the cigarette ash. The red jewel in the tip gleamed under the lamplight near us with the action. She stared at me for a hard minute, taking her time to draw in smoke from the stick and exhaled it in my face. Her tone was pitying. "Boy oh boy, are you screwed. You're right in the middle of this war and don't have a damn clue what it's over."

"Then, why don't you fill me in, sweetheart?"

She chuckled. "Well, my assessment's over. You're harmless." She threw her head over a shoulder and winked. "Come on. I know a guy who'll help you out, big cat. I think he goes by Ollie nowadays—"

"Ollie?" I froze. "You know Ollie?"

She backpedaled. "Do you?"

"He's my brother."

"Well, yeah, but if you know him, why the hell don't you know anything else? Hasn't he filled you in?"

I didn't like what she was suggesting. "Don't tell me he's part of any gang business."

"He always kept his nose out of it. Probably why he's one of the few of you I like. His sister's not so bad either, but I don't know if she's in town."

"He doesn't have a sister. *We* don't have a sister."

She cocked an eyebrow. "Have you been down here with Ollie this whole time?"

"What's it to you?"

She hummed, looking troubled as her ruby lips twisted. "In all that time, I would have thought he'd at least prepare you for the race. Do you even have a piece on you?"

"You've already been acquainted with it." I pulled back my lapel and motioned to the pistol holstered at my hip.

She groaned and massaged her eyes. "Lord, Ollie, what are you doing…" She let out a sharp breath and put a hand on her hip. "It's Alastor, right? Look. I'm going to be straight with you for a minute. I came down here from Chicago because Rhoda phoned me some weeks ago asking for help."

"And Rhoda is…?"

"Your brother's wife," she muttered. "You don't even know that much?"

"You must be thinking of some other Ollie, because his wife's name is Sun."

She waved a dismissive hand. "That's just the cheesy nickname he calls her. Romantic sap…" I thought I caught a glint of jealousy on her face, but it vanished when she shook her head. "Anyway, I came here to help your brother with a problem, and I'm guessing that problem extends to you, whether you know it or not."

"I think Ollie would have told me if he had a problem."

"Apparently, he doesn't tell you much of anything, does he?"

A loud *bang* sounded from the rooftops, and a second later, something shot through Dee's temple and burst out the other side. She dropped in an ungraceful slump, her smoking stick clattering to the cement beside her body. I cursed and ducked behind a parked car, getting out my pistol.

"That," came a man's voice from what sounded like a roof across the street. "Was for your little stunt in Virginia. Consider us even, little Miss Bone-Fucker."

I peeked over the car's hood. Dee's body was still where I left it, the red jewel from her smoking stick gleaming in the lamplight next to her head.

I scanned the roofs. It didn't take me long to find the shooter. And it didn't take him long to find me.

"Ah!" The pot-bellied, three foot dwarf pointed

his cane at me from the roof, chuckling. "There's the little roach."

Something wasn't right about the guy. Something about his… posture? Bone structure? What the hell was I looking at?

He sounded human enough, sure, but the cracked angle his elbows were bent in, jutting behind his curved spine and—I swear to god—*horned* shoulders, made him look like a god damn nightmare.

It looked like he had boney wings coming out of his ankles, two for each leg. I thought for sure I was seeing things, until the damned things flexed and gave a stretching flap.

No.

I rubbed my eyes, blinked hard, then looked again. The spiny wings and blackened horns were still there. They fluttered again, like a pair of disgusting bats.

No, no, no.

I rubbed harder until my sockets were stinging with pain and I was seeing stars under my lids. I took in a deep breath and looked again. The damn wings were still there.

What in the hell…?

The short-stack-demon-thing stepped off the ledge and, with a less than elegant display, those wings flapped and lunged his heavy weight to the ground. When he touched down, he nudged his cane against Dee's body.

"Clean through? Man, my aim's gotten better." He smiled wide and giggled like a school boy. Then he spotted her smoking stick and bent to pick it up.

He rolled it in his fingers, examining the red gem embedded in the centerpiece. "Getting sloppy, girl, and it ain't sexy."

He tapped his cane with delighted clicks and hummed a small tune while sucking in the smoke from the stick, walking my way. Crap.

I panicked and threw my arms on top of the sleek hood, aiming my gun at him. He didn't stop or even change direction. He just kept humming, doing a little jig each step of the way, his horned shoulders swaying and foot-wings twitching. Ew.

When he was close enough for me to see his tusks, my nerves squirmed and took over. I gave an undignified shriek and squeezed the trigger.

*Bang!*

His figure blurred left so quick I almost missed it with a single blink. Those damn wings had tucked themselves back beside his ankles, and he started on his merry way towards me again.

I panted, feeling my lungs ice over. *I'm seeing things. I'm fucking seeing things.*

Bang! Bang! Bang! I shot again and again, each time, the wings unfolded just when he would blur out of the way. And each time, he would keep strolling on as if nothing happened.

*Bang! Bang! Bang! Bang—Click, click, click, click, click...*

Out of bullets. And not one of them hit the freaky bastard. Before I could run for it, he zipped out of sight and I felt something cold shove against my back. Then a crunching crra-click sounded.

"Nice try, little roach," he said, and I could imagine the patronizing, tusk filled smile that came with the tone. "But that wouldn't have done anything anyway."

I swallowed, raised my hands. "What the hell are you?"

"You don't want to know. And you're not going to know anything anymore, so sorry. Nothing personal. Family stuff, get my drift?"

Bang!

I screamed at the pain that shocked through my shoulder—but it hadn't come from the back. It came from the front and burst *out* the back. The foreign bullet must have hit the midget demon behind me, because he cried out and the pressure on my spine vanished.

The pain in my shoulder swelled and burned, bringing me to my knees as tears blocked my vision. But there was someone there, someone on the roofs. I could only tell because a faint, blue glare was gleaming from the moon, and there was a shadow in its way.

I tried blinking away the water, squinting. Yeah, there was definitely someone there. And god damn it, they were just as much a freak-show as the first guy. Except... feminine.

Her silhouette gave the impression of a womanly figure, though misshapen and contorted in a mangled heap of limbs, long antlers, feathers and two extra appendages that sprouted from her back in a spiral.

The new nightmare peered down at me. I could only see it from this distance because her eyes gave off a silver glint, despite being on the wrong side of the moonlight. The thing stared for only a fraction of a lifetime, but it was enough to shock me stiff while she flexed her twisted wings, the long, scraggly feathers yielding to the wind, and made her way down to Mr. Midget-Freak and me.

In her graceless flight, I beheld the enormity of this beautiful terror's wingspan. Her longest feathers stretched to the length of a car-and-a-half, but wound in an awkward spiral from back to tip, white feathers speckled with black patches.

And they were coated in blood.

With that horror touching down just feet away from me in a puff of wind, I'd say it's no wonder I didn't notice the gun in her talon-filled hand. Not that it made a difference, my bladder still threatened to leak without the damn pistol.

But she moved the barrel away from my chest when the midget waddled out from behind me, his webbed face boiling—yes, boiling, like simmering rubber—as he seethed through his tusks and clutched his bleeding shoulder.

"What the hell are you doing here?" he sneered at the tall she-goblin.

He'd dropped his gun in the surprise—along with Dee's smoking stick, and his cane that was tucked under his arm—and all three items had skidded away from him. The gun and the stick rolled under the car by my feet, and with the sting in my shoulder fading, though not quick enough, and the two monsters distracted with each other, I was the only one who noticed.

"I should ask you the same." The woman—bird—thing had an over-toned, wavering voice, one that sounded like both a choir of angels and a war cry from Hell.

My first instinct was to give a shameless squeal and hightail it out of there, but now that she was under the streetlights, something about her feather-sprouted face made me pause. Sure, the white-and-black speckled hair matching her wings was wild and anything but normal, but then, it was tied in a polite braid. And her blue overcoat, though torn at the back and stained with blood, looked like it was from a fancy catalogue or outlet store. Which was weirdly human.

There was also something familiar about that face. Search me for why, but it was really familiar. But I sure as hell haven't seen this thing before. Her eyes glinted crystal blue, shining under white—well, one side white, one side black—lashes like silver moonlight, brow cast low and stern as she cocked her gun and aimed for the little goblin next to me, whose beady eyes had just found the gun under the car.

"*Min to kánete aftó, Ermís,*" she warned in Greek.

Confused as I was, I wasn't going to complain about the language change. There was something comforting in understanding what was being said, even if you didn't know what in hell was going on. And a simple message of "do not do this" was enough to tell me this demon-dame, at the very least, wasn't on this guy's side.

"*Gamísou,*" he spat in return, keeping to the Greek. "I see the Moon Mistress still can't keep her itching beak out of our business."

"The family is my business. What were you

going to do, after shooting our brother? Walk away with that piece and think we won't come after you?"

The guy's face was incredulous. "'Brother'?" He gestured to me with the arm that'd been shot. It seemed fine now. "This dirt kisser?"

The pain in my shoulder finally thudded into nothing, the wound sealing itself. I hurried to grab the guy's lost gun and Dee's smoking stick with the gem in it, clutching them tight in either hand. I didn't know what they wanted this thing for, but it had to be important, by the sound of it. Hell, Dee had just been killed for it. If that didn't scream 'crucial' then I may as well close my office and take up stamp collecting.

I stood between the two creatures, not exactly sure where to aim the pistol. I ended up picking the goblin who'd shot Dee, since this other gal seemed to want me alive, if not in one piece. I was more for that than being a nightmare's gamy meal.

I cocked the gun and barked. "*Kápoios na mou exigísei ti symvaínei!*"

Nobody moved. I raised the smoking stick and tried again, panting. "*Loipón?* Why do you want this thing? What is it?"

"It's mine," a third, familiar voice clipped behind me in the same language, and the stick was snatched out of my hand. The new voice went back to English, but the sound was distorted and crackling like embers. "Damn bastard got his spit all over it…"

Slowly, I looked back. Standing behind me and wiping the mouthpiece off with her skirt in a grumble was Dee.

... If, of course, Dee were a skeletal chimera whose suddenly fleshless face smoldered and split like coals over black fire, with creases of blue lava burning through the seams of her exposed skull. Her black hair flickered and smoked like soft flames, smoke curling from the tips and winding around her neck like a hazy necklace.

I almost dropped the gun, but by some miracle, I kept hold of it and thrust it at Dee instead. "Haahhh—ahhh—you—"

The last thing I heard was the cranking crrra-click of a gun cocking behind me, felt the metal push onto my head, and then a deafening bang! sounded before the pain surged through my head. And everything went dark.

**PART II**

# 4

The voices were a muffled blurb in my ears.

For a minute, I thought I was underwater, the way their tones waved in and out of focus. Then colors splashed and pulsed over the blackness with them. It wasn't a fully-defined scene, more like a wash of amber and red blurs, each shape fuzzy and not detailed. The hues were cluttered with static, which flickered and buzzed in the splotches of color as the scene surged like a highway route of veins, flashing bright then dim, bright then dim, bright then dim.

"What do you mean you didn't get the piece?" It was a woman's voice, coming from the brightest red blur in the center. There were two others surrounding her, and a third standing in back— behind me.

"I mean I didn't get it," a familiar voice said. Or had I said it? Something shifted in my brain, it was like my thoughts were being invaded by someone else's. I felt my mouth open, the words spewing out involuntarily. "The moon-bitch showed up and caused some trouble. And I apparently have a new brother?" Venom poisoned my voice. "When the hell did that happen? And why didn't you mention it?"

The woman-blur in front of me paused. "Oh? He was there?"

"God dammit, Ma!" A crash sounded when I threw something off the fuzzy desk. "Why didn't you say something?"

"I forgot," she said. Something clinked against glass, probably ice from a drink. "He was a tiny thing when your brother stole him from me. It was back when I nabbed your father's stash... I wonder... could he have been the one sending snoops after me yesterday? I tailed the last one I saw poking his nose around the opera. Found two men there, along with Miss Skeleton. Doesn't sound like a coincidence, does it?"

"Well, ain't that just a ray of god damn sunshine!" I yelled. "What the hell does he do? What's his talent? I swear to god, if we're up against another dream weaver, I say we get the fuck out of here while we can. I ain't going through the nightmares again."

My voice contorted and muffled into silence.

\*\*\*

When I woke up, my skull was blistering, but my thoughts were thankfully my own. Then I noticed my throat was dry and scratchy, my lungs burning like they hadn't been working in my sleep. I tried cracking open an eye, but only saw blackness, with the occasional red pulse still blinking like the lights of a cop car.

I would have thought I was outside, except there was jazz playing somewhere from a phonograph. There were also hushed voices coming from, what sounded like, a different room, and the smell of herbal tea perfumed the air. I could have sworn I heard Ollie's voice murmuring over there, sounding frustrated. Sun's voice came next, equally furious. I couldn't tell who they were talking to. There were too many voices to keep track of from here.

The glare of overhanging light on the ceiling came to view when the blackness started spotting away, slowly but steadily, and the blood in my veins started pumping again. My entire body, from head to toe, had been numb before this. So much that I could barely even feel my limbs. Now, with the blood rushing so quickly, a hailstorm of needle-like pricks washed over my skin, forcing a pained wail through my lips and gritting jaw.

Once I had my sight back, I recognized where I was. It was the living room in Ollie's house. I was on the couch. I tried moving my arms, and even though they worked fine, it hurt like hell to lift them, muscles singing with an intense burn as if I just took a long swim. More prickles swarmed down the limbs all the way to my fingers. Trying to ignore it, I rubbed my eyes, hands smearing down to my chin as I gave a sluggish, aching groan.

When did I get here?

I managed to push myself to a sitting position, joints and back popping in a sore symphony. My head started pounding again, and I leaned over my knees to breathe out hard, clutching my temples. I must have drank too much at the bar with Ollie and forgot I came here. Yeah. That sounded right. Still, that was one ugly dream. And this was one hell of a hangover.

When the thudding in my head subsided, I rose

and shuffled to the window by the television, peeling back the curtain with two fingers. It was raining. Flashes of light glowed from the dark sky as the water pattered against the glass in front of me, thunder rumbling.

Ollie's muffled voice rose from the parlor room's shut door, where the mumbling voices were arguing.

"What was he even doing there?" Ollie demanded.

"Looked like he came to take my piece," came a third, vaguely familiar voice. "Tried to make off with it. Your mother probably sent him, since she saw me last night."

"Damn it. Damn it, god fucking damn it…"

I made my way over, stopping at the door. There were a few *clinks* and the sound of billiard balls smacking beneath the hum of voices. When I cracked the door open, I peeked in and found Ollie standing at the back corner of the red-felt table, his hands waving in strict gestures. He wasn't happy. Sun was there, too, the pool cue in her hands as she lined the white ball with the yellow striped one and took a shot. She missed horribly, handing the cue to Ollie.

He snatched it up, barely flicked his eyes at the table, smacked the white cue with a single, swift stroke and clocked three solid balls into different pockets off the ricochet. He didn't acknowledge the impressive play and tossed the stick to a third player.

Dee.

And across from her was the dame from my

hangover-induced dream. But she looked different. Those horrifying wings, antlers and talon-like claws were gone, her white-and-black speckled hair now a faded brunette. It was still in a braid, lain over her shoulder. She wasn't wearing the coat anymore, and now wore a borrowed yellow blouse I recognized as Sun's.

Brunette took the pool cue when Dee was done and didn't bother looking at the table while making her move. The remaining balls were all smacked in their respective holes, and when the eight ball rolled itself in last, Sun and Dee let out annoyed grumbles, going to return the balls on the table to play a new game.

This picture wasn't making sense. Miss Brunette and Dee were there in the flesh, playing pool with my brother and his wife? Sure, they were having a heated argument, but bickering while playing a civil game of billiards? What the hell was going on?

I squinted at the four from my hiding place, noticing something wacky was going on with my vision. My eyes were having trouble focusing. Colorful filters started fuzzing over everyone. Dee had a splotch of blue over her image, Sun had a pink hue, and the other two had identical colors of red. I looked down at my hands, seeing they had the same red shade as the last two.

The colors flickered before disappearing, my eyes regaining focus. I rubbed my lids groggily. What did I hit my head on?

I went back to watching the four of them as Ollie sighed and rubbed his neck, the tension lessening from his shoulders. "Look, we're running out of time. You might have your own pieces, but we're down to just one." He glanced at Sun, who fingered the red necklace at her throat. "We have two kids now, so we need at least four more, if we're including Alastor—"

"Four more what?" I asked.

They all shut up to look at me when I opened the door fully.

"Al," Ollie hesitated, probably worried about how much I overheard. "Sorry. I didn't know you were awake."

Dee took the pool cue and lined up her shot. "It's about time, too," she smacked it, and the solid blue ball barely made it into a center pocket. "Was this your first time?"

"First time for what?" I asked.

Ollie shook his head. "Don't worry about it. The first time is always the hardest, and it takes more time to recover. The more it happens, the more your body will build up a tolerance."

The brunette snorted by the phonograph. "Still hurts, though."

Sun slapped the dame's shoulder, drawing fingers over her lips to tell her to zip it. Brunette only shrugged. "He's got to learn sometime. May as well be now."

"All right, enough with this cryptic crap." I pointed at Brunette. "Just who the hell are you? And why do you look like…" I thought about that, not sure who she looked like. It was on the tip of my tongue, but she definitely reminded me of someone I knew. Someone I knew well.

Ollie rolled his head back and massaged his neck, coughing into a hand. Then I noticed it, and pointed at my brother. "Him," I said. "You look like him. Except… a gal."

"Alastor," Ollie began carefully, gesturing to her unceremoniously. "This is Anita. She's my… sister." He coughed again. "Our sister."

My stare flattened. "We do have a sister?"

"Uh, yeah." He sniffed and rubbed a finger under his nose, a nervous tick of his. "I asked her to come down here and help us with a little problem."

"With Ma, you mean," I muttered. My gaze flicked to Dee. "Didn't you say Sun asked you to come down and help with whatever's going on, too? Or was that part of my dream?"

Ollie's brow was glistening with a small layer of sweat, which he rubbed with the back of his hand when he asked. "What dream?"

I waved a finger between Dee and Anita. "These two were in it. But they were freak shows, and some midget golem with wing-feet or whatever came down and…" I felt along the back of my head, where the faint ache was almost gone. It was still there, technically, but it was more of a memory than actual pain now.

"He shot me," I finally said.

Anita sneered. "Yeah. Ernie's a real ass sometimes. He wanted to distract us while he split, so we wouldn't follow him."

"You're saying it wasn't a dream?"

Dee sang a single note while chalking up the cue. "Bingo."

"I actually got shot? In the head?"

"Right through." Dee blew off the loose chalk, then bent over the table to line up her next shot. "Dropped like a sack of fish guts." *Click!* Her next shot missed the left corner by an inch. She handed the cue to Sun.

I glared at Dee. "Like you looked anymore elegant when you went down, toots," I hesitated. "Wait a damn minute—he shot you. I saw the bullet go straight in. Why the hell aren't you dead? Why aren't... we..."

She grinned as Anita hid a chuckle behind her hand.

Ollie licked his lips. "You can't die, Al."

"Excuse me?"

"You can't die," he said again, running a hand through his cropped hair. "None of us can."

I gave a light laugh. It faded when he didn't crack a smile, or admit he was joking. What the hell? "Everyone dies," I protested. "Especially after being shot. The bullet probably just grazed me—"

"Oh, for the love of..." Anita bent to unstrap something from her ankle. She rose again with a throwing knife in hand. "Watch closely."

Before I could ask what she was doing, she whipped the knife across the room at me. It whistled past my face when I ducked out of the way, and the next thing I knew, a squishy thunk sounded to my right, followed by a grunt. My neck wouldn't turn fast enough. The knife was sticking out of Ollie's right temple. He didn't even have time to gasp when his eyes went dim, and he slumped out of the chair onto the floor, the blood dripping down his jaw.

I screamed, adrenaline kicking in too late as I

hurried to Ollie, my hands shaking. I screamed again.

"Turn it down before you wake up the kids," Anita warned, dropping her throwing hand. "Amateur."

I leapt to my feet and took out my gun, aiming at her. "Who the fuck are you?!"

"Your sister," she said, examining her nails. "Weren't you listening?"

"You fucking killed him!"

"Yeah." She cocked an eyebrow. "So?"

"So I'm going to blow your goddamn—"

"Alastor."

My throat tightened.

"You're going to wake up the kids if you set that thing off in here."

I craned back, the lump in my lungs sticking. Ollie was sitting up on the floor, the bloody knife in his hand. His temple, though coated in red, was smooth and untouched. He got to his feet when I dropped the gun with a clatter.

Ollie rubbed at his temple and clicked his tongue after seeing the blood on his fingers. "Damn it, Anita," he said and glared at her, but only in annoyance. "Now I have to take another shower."

A smirk tugged her lips. "Then I'm doing all of us a fav—"

Ollie threw the knife right back at her, and it shoved into her forehead right between the eyebrows before I could blink. Her eyes lost lucidity and she dropped to the floor in a mess of tangled limbs.

"Sorry, what was that?" Ollie hummed as he

brushed off his sleeves. "I couldn't hear you over the sound of your ass hitting the floor."

I gawked at the new corpse, stiff where I stood. "Ollie, what the f—"

I leapt back when her hand twitched. After the next few twitches, a groan came from her lips, and her arm lifted to pluck out the knife with a flick of blood.

"At least your aim hasn't gone to crap," she muttered, pushing to her feet. She wiped the knife on her shirt and bent to slip it back into its holster at her ankle.

"What the hell?!" My throat swelled up, sweat rolling down my neck. The room was sweltering now.

Dee frowned at me from across the table. "Oh, now you've gone and scared the poor thing."

Ollie held out his hands in a 'stay calm' motion. "Al…"

The blood was still wet on his head, drip smears on his cheek and chin. I rushed out of the parlor and shoved open the bathroom door, squeaking on the faucet. I splashed my face with cold water, slapping myself a few times for good measure.

The floorboards creaked outside when I was rubbing my eyes, and Ollie mumbled. "Look, Al, sorry if that caught you off guard."

My laugh wasn't quite a whimper. "Off guard? You were fucking dead!"

"Only for a minute."

"Which is even worse!" I grabbed his head to look at where the knife wound should have been. "Right here? There was a knife lodged in here. I know we heal fast, but not from fatal fucking stab wounds. Or… shit, a landmine out at war? The letter was fucking right, wasn't it? You lost a leg."

He only shrugged, not denying it. "Limbs take a little longer to grow back, but…"

"Jesus Christ." I shoved past him, going to the front door. I threw it open to stalk out in the rain, away from these… whatever the hell they were. My own fucking brother—was he a demon freak, too? Christ.

Ollie followed after me. "Al, listen—"

"What the fuck is going on, Ollie?" I stopped in the wet grass and spun on my heels. "There are gargoyles walking around town, I get shot in the head, and you get a knife lodged in yours…"

"I know it's a lot to take in," he said, faint rumbles of thunder sounding overhead. "I guess you had to find out eventually. Come back inside and I'll try and explain."

"Explain now."

He pursed his lips, looking back to see the girls were hovering under the doorway. When he saw I wasn't moving, he shoved his hands in his pockets. "All right, fine. The four of us here, we're part of the Elders. We were some of the first to change on Mount Olympus—"

"Nope." I stomped onto the street. My finger was still pointing at him as I walked away. "If you're not going to be serious, then I'm just going to head home, get to my apartment, and get some damn sleep."

Ollie trotted after me. "Al—"

"No." I didn't stop walking as he caught up,

slowing his pace to stroll beside me. I waved a hand at his face. "No. This joke ends now."

"It's not a—"

"I think I'd remember living thousands of years and being hailed as a god."

"You weren't born then. Not everyone who's alive today were. Hell, Ernie was only born three Alignments ago, he was the youngest until you came along. And now Syrus and Cephísso are the most recent."

I felt the water soak through my clothes, dripping off my chin. "Wait. The kids are…?"

He nodded.

"Do they know?"

"They're not ready. And the next Alignment is happening soon, maybe in a few days. They won't survive if we throw them into this now."

"Survive?" I yelled at him, shoving him back. "You were just sitting there telling me we can't die!"

"We can't," he hesitated. "Except for a certain day."

"What day? When?"

"It only comes up every couple centuries. When three planets are in line."

"And then what? We all just up and die for good?"

"It's more complicated than that."

"How can this get any more goddamn complicated?"

He rolled his head back and groaned. "Boy, with *our* family? Extremely. Let's just say most of our siblings want to shut us in a box and bury us twenty feet under for the rest of eternity."

I spit out the rainwater that had blown into my mouth. "We have more siblings? But I… why haven't I ever met them?"

"Because I didn't want you to." His expression turned stern. "Most of them are insane. Sadistic. A bunch of psychos."

"Like you're any better?" I threw a hand at the house down the ways. "You and our dear sister over there were chucking knives at each other like it was a goddamn horse-shoe match. How's that for psychotic?"

He scratched his head, not able to answer. After a minute, he blew out from his nose and said. "Look, I'm not saying we're perfect either. I'm also not saying we're the 'good guys,' but we are the ones who want to keep you and my kids from being killed. And it looks like we might need your help with that."

"How am I supposed to help? I've never even met this other family, and if none of them can die— and none of *us* can die—then that seems like a bit of a stalemate, now doesn't it?"

"None of that will matter when the Alignment comes." His voice was grating. "Whoever doesn't have a piece will be torn apart by whoever has the biggest stash. And personally, I'd rather not be on the receiving end."

I would have argued that he was being vague again, but his hard stare made me think twice before opening my trap. He looked desperate now. Hell, he seemed downright scared shitless by whatever was coming.

"Please, Al." He squeezed my shoulder. "I don't want to see my kids die. Not again."

"Again? When did they die the first time?"

He shook his head. "I'll explain some other—"

He was cut off by a horn blaring behind us, the headlights we hadn't notice until now causing a glare through the rain as the car screeched and swerved...

The last thing I heard was a wet crunching sound.

*** 

"I'm going to find him, Sun," a faint voice washed through my eardrums. It sounded like Ollie. "I swear to god, I'm finding him this time. This has to be one of the biggest wars yet. If he's anywhere, I'd bet my piece he's in Germany."

All I could see were red and brown streaks, thumping in time with my heartbeat, drumming faster as the anger twisted and purred like an old friend.

My Sun's gentle voice came in a whisper. "And if you don't find him?"

"I will," I said, her face sharpening into focus as I slung my pack over a shoulder and headed out the door. "And when I do, I'll take back what's ours."

***

When the dream evaporated, that same prickling pain washed over my muscles when the blood rushed back. I thought I opened my eyes, but maybe

I hadn't. Everything was still black as coals.

I tried to wheeze air back in my lungs, but got a nose full of dirt instead. As my limbs slowly regained feeling, I squirmed to test control. My shoes kicked into something soggy on all sides, a wet weight pinning me down from head to toe. Where the hell was I?

My ears picked up a hushing noise overhead. It sounded like someone was digging. And crying.

Oh, damn.

"Mhnnhmnh…!" I yelled at whoever was up there shoveling more dirt over me, but the second I opened my teeth, the earth filled in the hole.

I heaved my arms up through the dirt—no, that was down, my palms were sliced by the rocks packed into the unearthed mud. I'd been thrown in here face down.

Sucking in more dirt as the panic set in, I dug my nails in the softer dirt that weighed down my head. Bit by bit, I crawled my way through the shifting chunks, then finally felt the cold, light air waft over my fingers.

A shriek cried out, and the sound of a shovel clattered to the ground.

My groping fingers finally found a solid purchase and I hauled myself up, gasping for sweet, clean breath.

There was a haggard woman shivering there, pale as a sheet and looking at me like she expected Hell's legion to follow me up here.

She wasn't making a move yet, so I folded my arms over the solid dirt to cough and catch my breath, the rest of my body still buried as I grunted.

"You got any smokes, lady?"

Her face wrenched into the darkest look of horror I'd ever seen in my damn life. She let out a gravely scream and hightailed it out of there, leaving one of her slippers stuck in the mud.

"Guess that's a no." I pulled the rest of me out of my shallow grave and flattened onto my back, panting.

It had apparently stopped raining since I was in there. This pet graveyard was thick with fog, and I heard the sound of cars howling and honking in the distance. I laid there for a minute, staring at the overcast and letting my lungs enjoy the taste of oxygen again.

A scratchy caw blurted from the left, and I rolled my head over the dirt. A beady-eyed crow was staring me down, its beak stretched close to my nose.

I went back to looking at the clouds and fished into my soaked coat pocket, pulling out my pack of Luckys and bit one between my teeth. I tried lighting it, but the thing was too wet from the rain, mud and blood spattered over it. I sighed, keeping it clamped in my mouth anyway.

The crow started pecking at my red-stained sleeve.

"I'm not dead, bub," I said. "Apparently, I ain't ever going to be. Find some other sorry sac to chew on."

My view of the clouds was obscured when Ollie showed up and peered down at me. "Well, that was interesting," the bastard muttered.

"Interesting," I echoed, still keeping the unlit

smoke between my teeth. "Yeah, that's what I'd call being buried alive. Interesting."

His head wavered. "Technically, you were dead when she dug the grave."

"Yeah, yeah. Wise guy." I took his extended hand and pulled to my feet, trying in vain to brush off the mud. "Does that mean you were there the whole time? Enjoy the show, you lazy bastard?"

He didn't try to hide his smirk. "That was my neighbor, Mrs. McDugal. She might not have recognized you, with most of your face now used as her new hood ornament, but if *I* showed up, she'd start asking questions."

I spat some extra dirt still in my mouth. "How convenient for you."

He rubbed his clean-shaven chin, looking at the messy grave. "Guess I know what kind of person she is now, huh? Got to be honest, I expected her to call the cops when she first hit you."

"Yeah, well, the old hag didn't, now did she?" I fished into *his* pockets and found his smokes and lighter, getting myself some of that smooth spice to settle my nerves. "You couldn't have just hauled me out of the street when it first happened?"

"You're heavier than you look."

"Heavier than I look?" I gave him a stink eye the devil himself would have flinched at. "The Almighty God of Athletics says I'm heavier than I look?"

"Maybe I could have hauled your ass out of there if it were daytime. But since it's the middle of the night, I don't have much more strength than your average Joe."

"What does the time of day have to do with any of that?"

"It has a lot to do with my talent." He rubbed a finger under his nose. "There's a reason they used to think of me as the god who brings up the sun. If it isn't out, my strength is sapped."

"Great. Now there's restrictions to these things." I sucked on my borrowed Marlboro, the end glowing orange, and sent a grey stream through my nose. "I think I've had enough dying for one night, Ollie." I sighed, exhaustion sucking me dry as I rubbed my sore neck. "Well. Not dying. Whichever."

That crow croaked at my foot, and I shooed it off with my leg. "And I've had enough of you feathered rats, too. Go on, get." The crow flew off, and I tugged my red-and-brown splattered lapel. "Damn scavengers, with those beady little eyes."

Ollie sighed and waved for me to follow him. "Come on. I'll take you home, I followed her with my car."

"Yeah, thanks…" I slicked back my hair, finding a piece of scrap metal wedged in my scalp, and plucked it out in a wince. "Say, there's something else I want to know."

Ollie looked back at me as I followed him, ready to listen.

"Your wife," I began, "her name's Rhoda?"

"Ah." He nodded to the side. "Yeah, that's what the others call her nowadays. Her real name's too long and it's not all that popular anymore. The shorter one is what she wanted to go with."

"Then why do you call her Sun?"

"Because she's my sun." His tone turned wistful as he smiled. "Bright and beautiful, she's the light that casts away the shadows of my heart; the ray of hope that gives me strength."

I snorted. "Was that the sappy line you used to get her to marry you?"

He winked. "You know it. But there's another reason for the name."

"And what is that?"

His grin was devilish. "Because, as they say, when Apollo shoots his arrow, the sun *comes* after."

The laughter burst out of me, both of us chortling on down the hill until we made it back to his car. After we shut the doors, I had an afterthought.

"Your sister," I said. "Our sister. Was I crazy, or was she actually some creepy gargoyle?"

Ollie cocked an eyebrow, then chuckled. "Let's save that for another time, Al."

"Do *you* turn into a…" I drew my lips into a line. "You know what? I don't want to know."

He couldn't hold back a laugh as he started up the engine and backed out of the driveway, wipers squeaking over the wet glass.

# 5

I fell asleep on the ride over and woke up the next morning in my apartment.

It wasn't a welcomed waking either, I couldn't ignore the annoying, ringing phone. After the fifth ring, I groaned and reached for it on the nightstand. I would have answered, but someone's clicking heels stalked over and beat me to the punch.

"Alastor Déus' residence, who may I ask is calling?"

My eyes shot open and I was out of bed in a jiffy.

"I see," the intruder—Dee—sighed into the receiver and blew out the smoke she'd inhaled from her cigarette stick, the curling wisps spilling out the open window she gazed out of. "I'll let him know. Thank you."

She put the phone back on the hook and turned to see me frozen stiff across from her. She hummed. "Hope you're ready to go. That was the captain. Earl, he called himself. He wants to see you in your office."

She started for the coat rack and grabbed her black hat, wrapping on the same colored jacket.

I glanced around the place, double checking that this was, without a doubt, my pad, and not someone else's.

"What the hell are you doing here?" I

demanded.

She slung her purse over her shoulder and reached inside to take out a mirror and a tube of lipstick, running it on her lips. "Ollie asked me to watch over you. Didn't want your mother coming in unexpected and making off with you in the night."

"Why did you answer my phone?"

"You're the one who called me your secretary, big cat." She shut the mirror and winked. "Just doing my job. Now why don't you show me this 'office' Captain Hunter mentioned? He's expecting you there in an hour."

She replaced the mirror and lipstick in her purse and started out the door that led to the apartment's stairwell. I checked over my clothes, noticing I was still in my drawers, but damn it all, the dame was already starting down the stairs.

I yanked open my dresser and wrestled with a set of clothes, grabbed my fedora from the rack and went after her. My footsteps clanked down the iron steps when I caught up, tying on my walnut-brown tie along the way.

"Listen here, doll," I said. "I can take care of myself, and I don't need some ancient, morbid skeleton to play babysitter in my own damn apartment without me knowing."

"What?" She grinned back at me when we reached the bottom. "Afraid I'm going to do something naughty while you sleep?"

My spine crawled. But, annoyingly, not in a bad way. She may have looked like a burning heap of bones last night, but now she was entirely human, down to the burnt cinnamon perfume tickling my nose. Hell, she was so mortal and fleshy it was hard not to imagine her without the dress.

*But she's still a damn skeleton under it all.* I glowered. Actually, now that I thought about it, weren't we all just that?

I shook off the thought, grimacing. That was beside the point. "Stay out of my place. Like I said, I can take care of myself."

"Might want this, then," she said, opening her purse and tossing me something—my gun.

I almost forgot I'd dropped it back at Ollie's last night. I fumbled to catch it, then holstered it at my side where it belonged as we stepped out to the streets. She chuckled after catching my glare and waited for me to take the lead.

"Where do we go from here, big cat?" she asked.

I glanced at the morning sky. The smell of last night's rain had gone stale, but the clouds still hung around to make sure a guy didn't get any ideas about feeling chipper.

"We," I said, "are going nowhere. I'm going to my office to meet Earl. You're going to run off and do whatever the hell you feel like, away from there."

"Why?" She kept pace as I stalked past her.

"Because…" I took a minute to think about it. Why didn't I want her there? I'd been set on questioning her for the last two days, but now the thought of her—or anyone else—hanging around just struck a nasty cord.

"I need a break from the circus," I finally answered. "I need contact with normal people."

"You mean people who can die when they're supposed to?" she offered.

I rubbed my eyes. "Yeah. Now scram, sugar. I'll head to Ollie's when I feel like playing."

I trailed off, spying something that interested me in the small bookstore to my left. "Stay here," I told her, and went in the shop. I purchased what I had my eye on and walked out with it in hand. I was so busy flipping through it, I forgot she was there and scowled at her. "I thought I told you to scram?"

"You also told me to stay here," she pointed out. "But remember, you told the captain I was your new secretary. He'll wonder why I'm not there."

"I'll tell him I fired you." I walked on, flipping through the book.

I heard her heels keeping up with me. "And what's your excuse for me being there this morning to answer your phone?" She got distracted with my choice of reading and asked instead, "What's that?"

I flipped another page. "Family tree, I guess."

She craned her head to see the title of the Greek Mythology text, and scoffed. "You won't find much, there. We've been rewritten and changed so many times I lost count after the 563rd version."

"Uh huh." I stopped on the next page. I pointed at the picture. "Is this supposed to be you?"

She glanced over, seeing the depiction of a boney skeleton with elf ears and a long, forked tongue in blue robes, summoning a ball of black fire in his hands. At his side was a three headed dog that looked just as hideous and vicious.

Her face contorted at the picture. "Who's the author?"

"Some wise guy named Ryan Bishop. Why?"

"Because I'm going to skewer him with a fire poker."

"You don't like the self-portrait?" I smirked.

"It's the ugliest I've seen yet."

"Well, that takes some kind of talent, doesn't it? If it's the worst out of 500 plus, I think he deserves some credit." I started reading the passage. "Why's it say you're a man? Or, demon-man? Why not a demon-woman?"

She wafted a hand in the air and crinkled her pixie nose. "At some point down the road, they were confusing me with a man named Persephonos. He and his mother popped up during the second Alignment—died on the third, the idiots—and he just so happened to have similar talents as me. Because of that bastard, everyone thought he was me, and that I was Persephone. Damn mortals never got it straight after that."

She started a new string of complaints, and I gave a tired yawn, flipping the page. My eyes were having trouble focusing. I glanced her way, and flinched. There was a light blue filter over her image, static fuzzing inside it. I could still see her features underneath, but they'd been sapped of their original color.

I massaged my eyes before checking her again. It was gone. But I could have sworn her black hair was now wavering unnaturally at her chin. It almost took the texture of fire.

I really needed to see an eye doc.

"So," I said, interrupting her mid-complaint. I hadn't been listening anyway. "What's your take on this 'war' thing? What do you want out of a family feud?"

"What I want is my own damn business," she huffed. Whatever I saw with her hair had gone away, the raven black strands laying normally at her chin again. "I was asked to help, so that's what I'm doing."

"But what's in it for you?"

"The hope of seeing your dear sweet mother taken down and staying down. I have a few scores to settle with her and her little Favorites."

"Mm-hmm. You have a thing for Ollie?"

She glared. "Think you got all the answers, don't you, Mr. Investigator? See, there's something he and Rhoda have that I want. But it's not something they can just hand over—it's that they know how to get it. They promised to tell me that little secret if I helped."

"And what secret is that?"

"Not yours to know." She turned up her chin, then gave me a sidelong glance. "Potentially."

"What'll make you spill?"

"Patience, big cat," she hummed, scrutinizing me from head to foot in consideration. "Let's just wait and see what your talent is, and what it'll offer in the war."

I hefted my shoulders, shutting the book and tucking it under an arm. "What's all this mumbo jumbo about talents you freaks keep yapping about, anyway?"

"Of course Ollie hasn't told you that, either." She rubbed her temple, then glanced at the grey, overcast sky.

I followed her gaze, seeing three crows were perched on one of the buildings next to us, their heads craned down and creepy little eyes watching us. Dee lifted a hand to them, pointed, then turned the finger over with an egging curl. The birds flapped off their roost and soared down to us. They came in a spiral, their black wings using the small breeze to carry them on their way. When they landed at Dee's feet, she bent and patted their heads.

"Well, one of you had an eventful day, haven't you, baby?" she said to the scruffiest bird, lifting its head by the beak and stroked its wings gingerly. "Eleven in one morning... weird."

"What are you doing?" I gagged, standing a good foot away from her and the feathered-rats. Disgusting things. No telling where those nasty beaks have been, or what old carcass they had for breakfast.

She looked up from the little goblins at me. "I'm counting today's tally. Boston's apparently changed in the last 200 years, especially its murder rate."

"So, they what? Tell you how many people died?"

"How many have been killed," she corrected, rising to her feet as the crows fluttered on their way. "Murders, suicides, accidental deaths—anything that isn't dying of age or sickness. And they don't just make a tally for me, they wake up the soul and tell them it's high time they made their exit."

"So, the birds do that for you?" I tried to hide my revulsion, but wasn't sure how convincing I was.

If she noticed, her shrug didn't show it. "Most times. I can't be everywhere at once. I have my gang to make impersonal visits for me if I'm not around. Besides, I don't usually handle personal appointments unless I know them, well, personally."

"And you only do this for people who've bit the bullet? Not the natural stuff?"

"The natural deaths don't need me to do anything. Their souls are already awake and take off on their own."

"I guess this is your talent, or whatever?"

She nodded, tone quieting while staring after the birds. "We all have something. It usually revolves around a specific theme, depending on our personalities."

"And your personality was just morbid enough to make you the Grim Reaper?"

"Apparently," she said and made a face that suggested it hadn't been a surprise. "I was an undertaker's daughter before this."

"That'd explain it all right." I rubbed my neck, not exactly comfortable with the subject, but boy was it too damn intriguing to stop. "So, why do you bother? Not that I don't think it's important, but it sounds like you all didn't get your, well, condition, till some incident. Did anyone do this Death gig before you?"

"I actually don't know. It's possible I'm the first."

"Then what happened to the people who didn't die naturally, before you came along?"

"Who knows? Maybe they're gone by now."

She took out her cigarette stick and pushed in a roll, then lit it—with the tip of her finger. No lighter. Just a quick *whoff* and bam: a smooth tear drop of fire slithered out of her finger. It wasn't a normal fire, either, it was a strange, translucent black color, with a tinge of blue in the center.

It almost made me jump back and scream, but luckily, all that came out was sudden gasp. "The hell!"

The cigarette flared red under the black fire, and she drew in a breath through the stick, humming out a wisp of smoke. "A party trick. Complements of my talent."

"What the hell does fire have to do with death?"

"Oh, I don't know." Her tone turned whimsical as she waved the stick. "I doubt there's a real meaning. Orpheus used to think it was something about 'life is as fickle as a dying flame' and 'once it's snuffed, it's the end of all things,' yadda, yadda... Wish I could remember the full thing. He was a lovely poet."

I paused. "Was? As in, not anymore?"

The corners of her lips sagged, then she rolled back her shoulders. "It's not something I like to remember. None of us do. And your mother doesn't seem to respect that, judging from that sentimental display she put together in the theater."

My feet skipped a beat, and I snatched her shoulder, spinning her around. "Wait a minute, doll. That message on the cello. It wasn't making a fable reference—it was about someone real. Someone you knew."

Her sigh was morose, spilling grey smoke that

stank of stale memories. "Yeah."

"Was he one of you?" I asked.

"One of us," she corrected. "In fact, he was more like you. Born into it, not changed."

"What happened to him?"

A pause.

I pushed. "Did he end up like our dead broad in the theater? Is that why it's arranged like that?"

Her teeth ground, and her shoulder jerked out of my grip as her heels clicked ahead. "How much farther is your office?" she asked.

She wasn't in the mood to squawk, then. Must have been hard to watch. Reluctantly, I let it go. "Just up ahead. Next two doors over."

It got awful quiet as we made it to the office and I unlocked the door. She followed me in when I flicked on the lights and plopped the mythology book on my desk.

"So, I got to ask," I began while taking off my coat and putting it on the hanger. I figured a slight change of subject would get her talking again, and even though I didn't want any freak-talk at the start, it was all getting too damn interesting to walk away. Not to mention relevant, now that I knew this Orpheus character wasn't just a storybook reference. But Dee obviously wasn't going to talk about that yet, so I had to coax her back into it. No telling how long it'd take, but I could wait. For now, I stuck with the easier questions. "If all you guys have these... what was it, talents? Do I get any?"

Dee glanced around the office with a crinkle in her nose. Must not have liked what she saw.

Granted, I wasn't exactly the best housekeeper, but it couldn't have been all that bad.

She let out a sigh and took a hit from her smoke. "Everyone gets a talent. For yours, it looks like we'll have to wait and see what it is. But one thing's guaranteed, whatever it is will reflect who you are, deep down." A grin stretched her lips. "So I guess, soon enough, we'll get to see just what you're made of, big daddy."

I lowered into my chair, folding my hands behind my head. "I just want to know if I turn into a hellspawn like the rest of you."

She shrugged. "You haven't yet."

"And thank God for that."

Dee checked over the room, left then right, and stopped at me. "How will my desk fit in this mess?"

My brow raised, scratching the stubble at my chin. I needed a shave. "What desk?"

"Mine." Her arms crossed, eyeing the left corner by the window, as if taking measurements at a glance. "We can't work in the same office with only one desk."

"You're right." I picked up yesterday's paper that had been on my desk. "Guess that means I can't have a secretary. Rotten luck, that." I flipped the page.

She sucked in a breath, probably ready to tell me otherwise, but the door swung open and set off the tinkling bell.

"Al," Captain Hunter blurted when he shut the door behind him. "What the hell were you thinking?"

I looked up from the paper. "Well, morning,

Earl. Good to see you too. What was I thinking about what?"

"About what?" he echoed and pushed his thick hands on my desk. "You damn well know what, and…"

He belatedly realized Dee was standing there, and she flashed him a smile. "Good morning, Earl. Can I get you some Joe? I saw an Italian Coffeehouse right across the street there."

He tugged at his collar and gave a less enthusiastic smile. "Uh, yeah. Sure, sugar. That sounds swell."

She nodded, shot a glare at me, and went on her way out the door and across the street.

When the door shut again, Earl looked around the room. Then he turned back to me. "Where's her desk?"

"Doesn't need one." I went back to the paper. "I'm firing her any—"

He swatted down the paper. "You damn well better not. Now you perk up your ears, son, or I'll rip them off. You better treat that gal right, and be damn sure to thank God she's even willing to work for a slob like you."

I scowled at him. "Why?"

"Because God knows you need a dame who knows how to answer the phone, Al. And not just professionally either. Don't think I didn't put two and two together when she answered the phone at your pad. It's about damn time you stuck with a gal and settled down."

I grimaced. "Get your thinker checked, Earl. That's not what's happening, and that's not why she was at my pad."

He snorted. "Sure it ain't. Either way, it'll be nice to clean up this pig sty. Maybe it'll look like a real office for once."

"How does it not look like a—"

"Get her a desk. And don't you even think of tossing her. If she isn't here the next time I walk in, there's going to be hell to pay, you hear?"

I slapped down the paper and propped an elbow on my desk. "Why'd you come in the first place, Earl?"

He snapped a finger, then his eyes flared bloody murder. "Mind telling me why you questioned Beckham about his little night of fun and didn't say a damn thing to me about it?"

*Beckham?* The name was familiar, but not by a lot. Beckham, Beckham…

Oh. The house director at the opera.

I tried to shrug it off. "I didn't think it was related."

"Not related?" he bellowed. "He was sleeping with the victim! How in hell is that not related? Christ, Al, this makes his wife a suspect, or even the other dame he was playing with the same god damn night! Now you kept that from me for a reason, don't think I'm an idiot. I've worked with you way too long. I know your habits. You know something about this case that you're not telling me, and you better spill it, Al, before I beat it out of you."

I made a show of stretching my back, the resulting cracks audible, then sighed. "All right, fine. The other dame he was with?"

He crossed his arms. "Yeah?"

"It was Henrietta. My dear old Ma."

He made a disgusted face. "You're joking."

"Don't I wish. Anyway." I glanced out the window, seeing Dee was on her way back with the coffee. She had three paper cups with her on a tray. I pursed my lips, not sure if this would be helpful or hurtful, but I didn't have any other ideas, so I said, "Dee was a witness."

His demeanor slacked. "Your secretary?"

"She saw me talking to Darryl before he was shot. She also got a good look at the killer—it matched the photo of my mother. I've been watching over Dee to be on the safe side, you know? And don't tell her I said anything, she was too scared to go to the police."

He nodded darkly, looking at Dee as she crossed the street toward us. "Can't blame her. Poor gal."

"Yeah," I muttered. "Anyway, I'll fill you in on the descriptions and testimonials soon. I'll get Dee to butter up to you guys in the meantime."

He nodded again, buying it, just as Dee stepped inside and handed us our steaming paper cups. "Here you go," she chirped with a smile at Earl. "Careful now, it's hot. Same for you, big cat."

Earl took his cup and grinned at her. "Thanks, sugar. 'Fraid I have to take this on the go, but you keep me posted if he upsets you. You hear?"

She chuckled. "I hear."

He started to leave, but stabbed a finger back at me. "Get her a desk."

The bell jingled on his way out.

I deflated into my chair, rubbing my stinging eyes. "Great. Now I have to keep up with filling

Earl in while sorting out my new freak-show family."

Dee perched herself on the edge of my desk. "Could be worse. At least you can't die. Yet."

"Well, if that doesn't lift my spirits, I guess nothing will." I slid my arms over the desk to rest my head. The mythology book's binding was at my nose now, and a thought played around in my noggin. "Talents reflect who you are, huh?"

I sat up and slid the book to the edge, pulling it open to the Contents section. I looked up the name I was wondering about and thumbed to the right page. "What's it say about Ollie?"

The book described all the basic stuff you hear about in school: sun god, shoots arrows, good at athletics, the model hero, blah, blah, blah… kind of a patron to the arts, something about loving music and poetry, and all that happy-go-lucky stuff… yeah, that sounded like Ollie. A real schmuck down to the core. The only difference I could find was the part where he got around. And I mean around. Apparently, most theologists couldn't seem to agree on which women he'd slept with, let alone how many. I idly wondered how much of it was true, and how much was a load of crap. The athletics and poetry stuff, I could get, but…

Wait.

I traced my finger along the line that mentioned which arts he was patron of. Then I went to a different chapter, pulling the book up to my face to get a closer look at it. Yep. There it was. And now, I suddenly realized the connection that I should have remembered from my earlier school years.

"Dee." I thumped the book closed and tucked it under my arm, rising to get my coat. "Bring the Joe and get your tail moving. I have to talk with Ollie."

"He's not home," she said.

My hand hovered over the knob when I glanced back at her. "How do you know?"

"He said last night he needed to see Heph."

"Who?"

"He's a friend." She paused. "Of sorts."

My stare flattened.

"He works for Ollie's side," she assured with raised hands. "Arms dealer. Ollie said he needed some extra protection."

"And this arms dealer just happens to live here in Boston?" I grunted.

"He flew up from Jersey a few nights ago, apparently. He called Ollie last night after he dropped you off and asked for a meeting."

"And where's this guy staying?"

She threw her head over a shoulder. "Last I heard, he'll be at the Golden Gals uptown in a couple hours."

"Then let's get to it." I opened the door, the bell giving its announcing tinkle. "We're going to crash a party."

"Sounds swell," someone piped in front of me. "Don't have too much fun, now."

I leapt back a foot, reaching for the gun at my hip.

It was the midget! The goblin from last night. Except now, he looked human, no disgusting bat wings on his ankles and no tusks in his mouth. But he was still three feet tall, so I guessed he was naturally a dwarf no matter what.

The squirt laughed at my reaction and propped his cane—which from this close distance I could now see had intertwined snakes and a pair of wings etched at the gold head—over his shoulder. "Jumpy. Good. An alert guy is a smart guy. Marks a survivor, so you at least got that going for you." His eyes moved to my pistol. "No point in that, though. We ain't here to play."

"We?" I glanced behind him, seeing there was a woman waiting there. Two guns were strapped on either side of her hips, fully visible since she didn't wear a coat. She clearly wanted to show she was armed. Aw, hell.

Dee stepped up beside me, and I noticed her grip on the smoking stick tighten. "I see you brought backup this time," she said in Greek, looking at the woman. "Hello, Anna. Here for the family reunion? Or are you also going to shoot me and steal my piece, like this little worm?"

I blinked at her, seeing the black strands of hair beside her chin had started wavering. It'd taken on a new texture, looking more like fire than hair. Black fire. With blue sparks. It was starting to dawn on me that maybe my eyes were working fine after all. Not that it was much of a comfort.

The woman, Anna, scoffed. "Your piece isn't going anywhere." This was in Greek. "We've got orders. We're here to give a message to Alastor."

Hearing my name come from someone I didn't know was unsettling as hell. I wasn't sure what I was supposed to say except, "What?"

The dwarf waddled up to me, and I took a step

back. He pulled out a piece of paper from his pocket, tossing it at my feet.

"Ma wants to know how you're doing," he said in English, then turned to leave with the woman. "Stop in and say hello. And don't be late."

They walked away, not even bothering to turn or check their blinders. There was something weird going on with their colors as they went. My eyes started to unfocus, and red filters spilled over them like a static-ridden film. They were both the same color. I looked at my hands. Same color. Dee, though? She was the only one with a pale, blue hue.

My vision refocused when the two turned a corner, and my brow furrowed. "Don't tell me. That other gal was my sister."

Dee snorted. "What gave it away? The family resemblance?"

"Something like that."

Dee's head turned to me in question, probably picking up on my tone. "What is it?"

I thought of how best to answer, licking my lips. "Do you ever get this thing where, if you unfocus your eyes, you start seeing… different?"

Her lids turned into slits. "Different how?"

"Like there are filters over people. And they each look a little different from the rest."

"Are you talking about Death Tones?"

"Death Tones?"

"The little splotches that cover people, like a film of static that spreads over them."

"Yeah." I pointed. "That. What is that?"

"Death Tones are found on everyone. They're clearer if someone has a long way to go before they die, and then slowly gets into a darker grey when they get close, and then black when it's days away."

"What do the different colors mean, though?"

She frowned. "Colors?"

"Yeah. Those two had more of a red tone, and yours was more bluish."

"There are no 'colors' in Death Tones, big cat. Only clear, grey and black. And they aren't found on immortals. We can't die, so we're never close to death."

"So what the hell am I seeing?"

She tapped the mouthpiece of her stick over a tooth, thinking. "Maybe something similar. But definitely something to do with your talent, is my guess."

I scratched an ear. "I don't expect there are tones for family ties, are there? To tell who's related to whom?"

"I don't see why not." Her brow raised. "I haven't heard of anything like that, though."

I blew out a breath from my nose, looking at the paper the dwarf had thrown at my feet. I picked it up. There was an address and a time written down, set for an hour.

"Crap," I muttered, pocketing the note. "Come on, doll. Our schedule's been crunched. And Ollie doesn't know his appointment's about to be interrupted by the family reunion."

# PART III

# 6

The club's singer cooed from the back stage as the saxophone's grizzly rasping danced with her vocal cords.

Golden Gals wasn't a place I was unfamiliar with. It had a bit of a reputation, with more than just having good looking broads and drinks so strong they tore through your liver like thorn-ridden silk. There was a small casino in the basement where I tended to hang around, get some of my informants to talk over drinks and a game of roulette. Since I wasn't technically a copper—well, not anymore—they usually let me in without any problems. Not to mention, the owner was a friend of mine. And on some occasions, she'd been a little something more in the private rooms.

It was a sparse night, at least on the main floor. Only a handful of fellas were at the tables, with just as many gals on the job. I guided Dee to the door that led to the cellar stairway, and was stopped by an unfamiliar, wide shouldered bouncer sitting slouched on a stool.

"No entry." He bit into the apple in his hand. "Staff only."

"Right." I folded my arms. "You must be new here. Name's Alastor. I'm a regular down there."

"I'll just bet you are." He took another bite of his apple, then restated. "Staff only."

I was ripe to tell him off, but a velvety purr interrupted. "Johnny boy, what have I told you about snacking on the job?"

He nearly choked on the slice he'd been working on and shot to his feet. "S-sorry, ma'am."

I smirked when turning around, tipping my hat to the red haired beauty. "Ariel."

The owner's bright red lips gave an inviting grin. "Alastor. Haven't seen your likes round these parts in a while. Been busy?"

"You could say that."

"Mmm." Her emerald eyes gave an intoxicating leer. "From what I hear, you've had one hell of a weekend."

I frowned. "What have you heard, exactly?"

Her throat gave a husky chuckle as she pressed a manicured nail to her lips. "Enough." Her glance slid to Dee. "Why, if it isn't Miss Dee herself. Been a few hundred years. Guess you didn't have time to swing by a girlfriend's pad and stop for gossip?"

Dee blew out a stream of smoke after taking a hit, then put a hand on her hip. "Sorry, Ariel. Duty often calls, or whatever excuse makes you feel better. I just haven't been in the mood for hysteria. But, I got to say, this place is pretty snazzy."

"You like it?" She gave an ostentatious wave of her hands, motioning to the joint like a showgirl advertising a new car. "It was a rough start, I'll admit, but I think it turned out wonderfully."

"Wonderfully," Dee mimicked, seeming to roll the description around on her tongue to see how it tasted. "Sure."

I groaned and rubbed my eyes. "Of course

you're one of them. Do I know anyone who can die when they're supposed to?"

Ariel shrugged her tan shoulders. "Sorry, honey. Ollie asked me to keep a lid on everything when you two first came down here. But I guess those rules are out the window now, aren't they?" She giggled, biting her thumb to try and hide her amused smile. "Heard you had your first accident. How'd it feel?"

"Like someone shot me in the head," I muttered, glaring at the bouncer who was still standing stiff and confused at the door. I threw my head one way. "Scram."

He hesitated, then looked at Ariel, who threw her head the same way, and he skirted toward the bar.

Now that Mr. Muscle was out of the way, I shoved open the stairwell door and headed down, Ariel and Dee following behind. The music from upstairs reverberated behind the door above us and slowly died the further down we went. It was replaced by different, more lively music now as we neared the bottom.

The smoke was a thick layer of haze down here, and the noise just as sweltering. The dim lights overhead were spotted and radiant in the musk, not bright enough to see each face in the room, but not dark enough to mistake your wife for the mistress you've been playing around with. The place was more packed than upstairs, and the various sounds of ice clinking in glasses, men yelling over the black jack and roulette tables, and the occasional thumping and muffled moans in the private rooms to the side all collected in a massive heap of chatter. The rattle of Billiards could be heard smacking from the tables in the back right corner, which is where I managed to spot Ollie through the grey haze.

I pushed my way over, seeing Ollie was here with Anita and one other character I didn't recognize. That one had to be this Heph guy Dee mentioned earlier.

He was a meaty one, stacked with muscle and a thick black beard and bushy eyebrows. His hair was slicked back with oil and his neck was so thick it made his head look too small by comparison. As he chatted with Ollie, he was going through a collection of different guns and ammo that was stuffed in a duffle bag on a spare chair.

As I got closer, I could just overhear the end of their conversation.

"And what exactly does he want us to do about it?" Ollie grunted in Greek while taking a shot at the pool table. The cue jumped off the felt and soared over a solid yellow ball, then arced down in time to smack both the green and blue stripes, and dropped both of them in separate pockets. "We've been trying to find that damn stash for years, and we keep coming up empty. And now all of a sudden, with the next Alignment on our hides, he thinks he can come in and find it just like that? It's not even his to take."

"It's not yours either," said the built man in the same tongue, taking the cigar from between his teeth. "Who says you have any more right to it than the rest of us?"

"*I* say." Ollie jabbed a thumb at his chest. "Rhoda and I have a family of four, plus Alastor, which makes five. One piece isn't enough for all of us. We need that stash."

"As do we." He flicked the ash away from his cigar. "In case you forgot, Henrietta took off with our own stash a while back. We only have two right now, and there's an entire organization for us to keep alive. Now you tell me how your personal needs outweigh the gang's?"

"It's not a matter of need, it's matter of right. That stash belongs to Rhoda and me, and you damn well know—"

"*Agória, Agória*," Ariel called and stepped in, tossing her hips along the way as she propped an arm over the table. She continued in English. "Watch your temper, boys. This is neutral ground, remember?"

Ollie glared at her, but looked past her to see me. "Al." He walked over. "What the hell are you doing here?"

"I'm here for a couple reasons," I said. "I was going to ask you a few things, but then something more pressing came up. We have to get out of here."

His shoulders tensed. "Why?"

"Because—"

"Alastor, I take it?" a woman asked behind me. It wasn't Dee or Ariel. The tone was wistful and impatient, a voice of authority that, despite the years I've spent away from it, I still recognized.

And Ollie's sudden iced-over limbs confirmed it. I took my time to turn around, my growl coming out thick and clear. "Ma."

The woman herself, standing before me and creasing her face with a withered smile while holding her violet smoking stick to her lips, sighed. "My, how you've grown. I only wish I could have been there to see it." Her edged gaze snapped to Ollie. "If only you hadn't been stolen from me, that is."

I reached for my gun, but Ollie held my hand down. "No, Al," he ordered. "Not here. It's neutral ground."

"Neutral ground my ass!" I struggled against him to get the gun out. I wasn't winning. "Dead broad and my late informant aside, she killed Pops! Or did you forget that?"

A hefty laugh came from the pool table next to us, where a silver haired man in a black fedora was just finishing a shot at the billiards. His back was facing us when he sucked on his cigar and breathed out a cloud.

"Oh, I don't think any of us forgot that," he said in a deep, throaty timbre, turning around to lean against his table, the rim of his hat tipped towards his sharp nose. His lightning-blue eyes still seemed to shine from under the shade. "She's done it so many times, I've lost count. But thanks for the worry, Al. It warms this old man's heart to see he's thought after."

My brain turned to mush when he stepped past me and went to look Henrietta in the eye. "Evening, dearest." His smile told of the unfinished scores that needed settling. "Hope you missed me. Now, if you'd be so kind as to keep your damn hands off our son?"

# 7

You know, in the investigating business, us sleuthing types like to think we're pretty good at connecting the dots. For instance, when you have a basic string of logic like, say, when you discover your brother couldn't die, and you couldn't die, and your mother couldn't die, then didn't it stand to reason that, of course, your father couldn't die, either? And that, if said immortal father was thought to have been shot by said immortal mother, it also stood to reason that he just got back up and went on his, no pun intended, mother fucking way.

But wouldn't you know, the thought never came to mind. Because apparently, I was a goddamn idiot. So here I was, standing right in front of a man I thought was dead for over 40 years as he confronted the woman I thought had killed him. What the hell was I supposed to say?

Either way, I just stood there. So did they, except neither were paying me any attention. They were too busy sharing daggered looks.

Henrietta was the first to break the silence. "I thought I smelled something rotten in the storm last night. New cologne?"

He grinned. "Thought you'd like it."

"Dear, sewer rats would flee to the nearest shithole."

"Then I'm lucky to have married a swine who

appreciates it. Why are you here, Hera?"

She thrust her chin over at me. "I wanted a few words with our son. And you?"

"Same reason. Except he's under my protection. So, if you wouldn't mind skedaddling?"

She bristled. "*Your* protection? You haven't seen him since that bastard son of ours stole him, either."

"You forget." His voice grew dark. "That bastard son is one of my favorites. And my favorite daughter's here to back him up. They both have claim of our youngest here, and since I have claim of both of them, that claim extends to Al."

She gritted her teeth as her grip on the smoking stick almost made it snap in two, but said nothing.

"Beat it, honey," he said. "I made an appointment, and you're interrupting. Or would you rather trade lead on neutral ground?"

Ariel snapped. "Do, and you and your businesses aren't welcome here anymore. Either of you. And I can't promise your own organizations won't run into a little… accident."

In her hands came a strange, radiant glow, a stream of smoky gold light weaving over her palm and producing an apple. She set her teeth against it, making them jerk forward with protesting shouts.

Henrietta's eyes were smoldering now, and after checking over our numbers, which outmatched her own, she blew out a huff and spun on her heels. "Fine. I'll wait my turn. But keep in mind, Alsastor." Her gaze flared at me. "We have the most pieces to offer. Stay with them, and I can guarantee you'll be choking on soil come next

Alignment."

She waved for her company to follow her out, and they went up the stairs with Ariel as a threatening escort.

Pops rubbed his beard while staring after them. "Looks like we'll need to be careful, coming out of here."

"We'll go out the back way," said Ollie, leaning against the pool table and downing a glass of whiskey that was set there. "Hope you and Heph have a place to stay the night. With Anita here, Rhoda and I have a full house."

"We haven't been in Boston long enough to look." Pops stroked his silver beard and looked at me. "What about you, Al? Any room for your old man at your pad?"

I stared at him.

Whatever expression I had made his brow furrow, and he asked. "Cat got your tongue, Al? Now I know it's been a while, but you got to remember your brother hid you for a while there. I would have come to say howdy if I knew where you both were."

My brain failed to come up with a reply again.

"Al?" He lifted a hand, reaching for my shoulder.

I slid away from the gesture, my tone guarded. "You're alive."

He looked at Ollie, who shrugged. When Pops turned back to me, he said, "Yeah. And so are the rest of us. So what?"

When I couldn't think up a response that made any sense, Ollie answered for me. "He saw Ma kill you, so I just stuck with that story."

"Well isn't that just a god damn cherry on top?" He shook his head. "No wonder he looks like Dee on a bad day. Al, look. I'm obviously not dead, so might as well get over it."

"Get over it?" I yelled, finding my voice again. "I spent 42 fucking years thinking you were dead, and just as long hunting down that woman!" I pointed to the stairs. "To give your damn name justice. So, now I find out my lifelong vendetta was for goddamn nothing, and you tell me to get over it?"

He fanned a hand to his chest. "You held a grudge that long for me? Al, I'm touched."

"Shut the fuck up. If you weren't dead, where the hell have you been?"

"In Jersey." He shrugged. "Running my business. A business that your brother apparently doesn't care about."

Ollie scowled. "I have a family, Pops. One that I want to keep alive this time around. We can't afford to give up any pieces we come across just because you want to recruit your casino goons."

"You wouldn't have to give up all of the stash. Here, since we're both hunting for the same thing, why don't we split a deal?" He leaned back against the neighboring billiard table and propped his elbows on the edge, flicking ashes off his cigar. "If either of us finds the stash, you'll get the four pieces you want, and we get the rest. Fair?"

Ollie glared at him long and hard, lighting a smoke in silence. The chatter buzzed around us as he waited with his answer, taking a swig of whiskey before slamming it down.

"Fine. Deal." Ollie clasped hands with Pops, though begrudgingly. "But I'm holding you to it. That stash belonged to Orpheus, and therefore now belongs to me, so you're damn lucky I'm not demanding the entire thing."

I straightened, snapping a finger at Ollie. "That's right—that's what I wanted to talk to you about: this Orpheus character…"

Ollie tensed. "What?"

"It came up at work. Ma carved up a broad the other day and put her out on display, and the name Orpheus was scratched on the cello she was tied to. I thought it was a fable reference at first, but Dee mentioned he was a real guy. And I want to know if the history in those stories is right."

He ran a hand through his hair, taking a drink. "Which part?"

"The part that says Orpheus was the son of Apollo. Your son."

He stared at me, then with a hard sigh, he nodded for the back doors. "Guess I've waited to tell you this long enough. Come with me."

# 8

Ollie brought us back to his home, leading us to the attic while Rhoda cooked dinner with the kids downstairs, Heph offering to help her.

I thought it was weird that this large, burly stranger made a complete 180 on his stern glare when seeing Rhoda. They hugged like old friends, kissed cheeks while offering kind greetings, and the guy even put on a soft face for Syrus and little Stephanie. Rhoda introduced him as their uncle Heph. I wondered if he actually was their uncle. At this point, it wouldn't surprise me. Hell, I'd find it comforting, too. Having a thick necked, muscly arms dealer for a brother—why the hell not?

From up here in the attic, I could hear the clatter of pots and the sizzle of steaming oil on cookware under the floorboards as Ollie brushed away cobwebs from the wooden webbings. I followed him to the back corner, Dee, Anita and Pops trailing me.

There was a large, dusty trunk locked up in the back, an antique-looking chest with cast iron handles and bearings. It was so old, the wood seemed to be rotting off, and a metal plate was nailed at the front. It wasn't until Ollie rubbed away the coat of dust that I saw the engraving on the plate: *Thymitheíte Orféa.*

It was the same thing scratched into the cello at

the opera house.

*Remember Orpheus…*

"How long has this been here?" I asked, crouching next to Ollie as he stared at the plate with stale eyes.

I'd lived here for most of my damn life, growing up. Hell, I'd even been in this attic before. I faintly recalled seeing this same trunk when I was a kid, and asked Ollie what was in it, but he never offered an explanation. He kept it locked up with that rusted old pad, too, so busting it open wasn't going to happen without either a key or a pair of bolt cutters. Not that I was old enough at the time to know what the latter was.

Ollie let loose a smooth stream of breath through his nose, brushing his fingers over the engraved plate. "It's been… a long time, Al. A very long time."

Pops spat behind me. "Not long enough. Your mother seems set on shoving it back in our faces this coming Alignment. We've barely had time to mourn."

Anita and Dee were silent, both women looking ripe to snap someone's spine in two. Dee's hair was wavering like black fire again, and her cheeks were looking a bit on the boney side.

Ollie was the only one who looked blank. He unlocked the trunk with a key strung up on a chain around his neck, where it had been hidden in his shirt. How long has he been wearing that?

When the lid was lifted with a soft squeal and Ollie swiped away the thick string of webs, I peeked over his shoulder to see all the books, loose papers and random trinkets piled inside. It wasn't a very neat pile, I guessed some things had been thrown around when it was moved up here. Then again, there was no telling where it'd been before this. Ollie obviously had a life before I came along, hundreds of lives, it looked like. I'd have to ask him about all that some time.

Ollie rifled through the paraphernalia inside and soon pulled out a thick, banged up journal. The yellowed pages looked ripped at the edges, some had even come loose and were sticking out at the corners. Ollie took a long minute to study the dusty thing before peeling open the cover and flipping through the tome.

The lettering inside was scribed with black ink and pen, the cursive so pristine and beautiful you'd think it belonged to a master calligrapher. As for the content, it looked like poetry. Maybe songs? It was a fancy, curling script that seemed to be from the colonial times. There were a few splotches of spilt ink every other page or so, and I wondered if those blemishes were from a bumpy wagon ride or a sloshing journey on a ship, given the rippling water stains on some pages.

But it wasn't all just written words. There were sketches here too, made with graphite or charcoal. Most were human portraits, of the finest detail and depth I'd ever seen in a single book. The black and white figures almost seemed to jump out of the damn page they were so tangible.

Ollie paused at one page with a drawing of a young man, his wavy hair grown to his shoulders and sideburns lining his jaw. He stood at attention in a military pose, saber drawn up and tucked at his side with the delicate hilt wrapped around his gloved fist. He wore an old fashioned, general's uniform, with tasseled shoulder pads and a broad lapel decorated with various medals of rank. This guy was a true vision of strength and justice, of duty and determination. It looked like a guy you'd follow into battle without a second thought.

It was also my brother.

There was a note off to the side of the portrait that read "Father, the face of freedom" and stated the date of the picture's creation. It was in the late 1700s. Jesus.

Ollie chuckled, as if remembering the day, and flipped the page. "I almost forgot about the sideburn era. What were we thinking?"

Dee grinned to his other side. "I don't know, Ollie. I think you pulled it off all right."

Anita snorted from a support beam behind me. "Better to have sideburns than be forced to wear those damned corsets. We couldn't breathe worth a crap, not to mention always having to buy new ones."

Dee shrugged. "I never had to."

"Because you have the luxury of not growing wings when you Change," Anita snapped.

"Luxury?" huffed Dee. "Being grounded at all times? I'm so lucky."

Ollie continued to flip through the journal. There were more sketches inside, masterpieces in their own right. I found one of Rhoda, even one of, I think, Dee crouching in a flower patch, reaching for a butterfly. It was an oddly serene moment to capture her in. She wore a black dress that was cinched at the waist and tied with a bow in the back, the long skirt flowing over the bed of flowers as she held a lacey parasol over her head, casting herself in shade from the beaming sunlight around her. She also had long hair dangling down to her chest. I wondered what made her decide to bob it. Was it just the fashion change between eras?

There was a poem written below the scene, and I squinted to read it.

*To wilt and bloom alike as one,*
*To seize the light outside the dark,*
*Be not afraid of love and laughter,*
*For Death doth too think life the master*

Dee sighed when reading it over Ollie's shoulder. "Such a sap, that kid…"

Ollie smiled thinly. "You always did inspire him. And it wasn't a wonder, since your talent was the strangest of all of us."

I scratched my gruff chin. "I don't get it. If I had a nephew who could do beautiful works like this, who'd want to… well, do what they did to him?"

Ollie's smile faded, looking up at me. "I've been trying to answer that for damn near 200 years, Al. And I don't know, even still. I never understood Aron. I don't think I ever will. His mind is just so… warped."

"And Aron is…?"

Anita scowled behind me, fingers tight on her arm as long talons grew from her nails. "One of Ma's Favorites. She always picked the selfish psychopaths who never gave a damn about anyone."

I grimaced. "So, he's our brother?"

Pops grunted. "If you want to still call him that, sure. I disowned him a long time ago, before your mother picked him up as her favorite. Even before the Change, he was demented. I caught the signs early when he was a squirt, torturing hounds and snapping the heads off of our carrier pigeons. He liked to draw on the wall with their stubbed necks afterwards. Kid was a damn lunatic. I thought we should put him down back then, but your Ma just thought he needed codling. Great help that did."

"So he just decided to kill his nephew for fun?" I asked. "Randomly?"

"It wasn't quite random," Ollie murmured, flipping the page in the journal.

A new woman I didn't recognize was drawn on the page, splashed with graceful blotches of watercolor paints to give life to the red-skinned figure and her native clothing. This was in more detail than any of the others.

She looked like a goddess, with a long, black braid that tumbled past her swollen bosom and a face so smooth and sculpted you'd think she were carved out of marble. Her dark eyes were wide and almond shaped, lashes curling from those sharp corners as raven feathers dangled from the leather band braided around her crown.

"Who's that broad?" I asked.

Ollie smiled. "Orpheus' wife."

Dee sighed, taking a seat on a dusty stool. "She was one of us. Apparently, Greece wasn't the only place to get an asteroid of pieces dumped on them. The Americas had a similar fallen star as ours, hell, maybe even a broken portion of the same one, and changed the indigenous people who grabbed it first."

"So that's what this is about," I muttered, getting out a smoke and lighting it. "Falling stars?"

"Pieces of them," Anita corrected, leaning against a support beam. "Shards that were scattered when the asteroid split from impact. That first night, they shined so brilliantly, we all first thought we were rich… But the minute we grabbed them, bam. And here we are."

Dee summoned a teardrop of black fire over her finger and lit her own smoke in her stick. "We didn't know what was going on, at the time," she explained in wistful reminiscence. "All we knew for that first 24 hours was pain. Our skin split and burned, our eyes melted in our sockets—well, mine did—some of us grew extra limbs. Basically, our whole genetic makeup was shifting from the inside out. We thought we were cursed for laying hands on the Gods' treasure, and were being punished."

"We basically became the damned." Pops' laugh was mischievous. "Oh, you should've seen the villagers' faces. Everyone feared us, especially with the talents we got from our new forms. They all started worshiping us as the Gods themselves. But, well, that only lasted so long. Different times. Nowadays, you couldn't get away with that."

"Uh huh," I grunted. "So what's the hype over having these pieces now? Sounds like the hunt's already over."

Ollie answered that one. "Not quite. Every 200 years, the pieces get their power restored with the planets' alignment. Anyone with a piece during these 24 hours either keeps their talents and forms, or gains it. Those without one, well… they lose it all. They become mortal again. And those of *our* family, particularly, are then susceptible to the wrath of our kin."

I nodded grimly, taking a hit from my smoke. "Which I guess is what happened to Orpheus?"

Ollie rifled through the journal again, each page now showing the same native woman over and over. Then he thumped it closed and whispered. "Yeah."

Dee let out a stream of smoke. "He went up against Aron. We tried to help. It seemed like a simple plan: gang up on Aron, take his piece during the Alignment and kill the bastard. Needless to say, it didn't work out so well. Aron is a force not easily matched, not even when outnumbered. He slaughtered all of us—it was a miracle our own pieces weren't taken—and thought it would be fun to use Orpheus as his own sculpture project. He stole Orpheus's prized violin and cut out the piece embedded in the wood. Then he ripped his head off and skewered it to the thing to make an example for the rest of us."

Ollie's voice was quiet. "Aron disappeared after that. I've been looking for him ever since, joining any number of wars I could, since he was usually playing in them, like some sick sport. If he's here…" His hands gripped the journal until his knuckles bled white. "I'm going to kill him."

"Unless he kills us first," Dee muttered. "We were squashed the last time we tried for him. He'll probably do it again unless we have a better tactic.

Or more people."

"We do have more people." Ollie flashed a glance at me.

My tone flattened. "I don't change into a demon. Hell, I don't have any talents, what am I going to do for you?"

"Don't be too quick to write yourself off." Pops crossed his arms. "We just have to figure out how to trigger your stuff. Who knows? You might just be the asset we've been waiting for."

"And if I end up being nothing?"

"Better to try than sit around and die," said Ollie. He held the book out for me. "There's at least one thing you can do, without any of that."

I took the journal. "And what's that?"

"You can find where my son hid his stash of pieces. We're not sure how many there were exactly, but we know he had some collection of them after he killed Morpheus and stopped him from wiping the rest of us out."

"Christ, you keep throwing out a new name every minute. Who was this guy, then?"

Dee grimaced. "Morpheus was a nightmare. Literally."

"Tyrannical Lord of All Bastards, I call him," muttered Pops. "Tried to hitch himself up as our king. And he was a tricky son of a bitch. He'd get us in our sleep, mostly, pry out our worst fears and bring them to life, slaughtering most of our kind and stealing our pieces. If Orpheus hadn't turned his nightmares back on him with his music, we all wouldn't be here now."

Anita drummed her fingers on her arm.

"Orpheus took the stash that bastard left behind, but he didn't think anyone should have so many in his possession. The more pieces you have during an Alignment, the more power your talents have until the next one. The minute Orpheus got the stash, he shut it up somewhere here in Boston, and never told a soul exactly where."

I flipped open the journal. "And you think I'm going to find it when none of you could?"

Ollie shrugged. "We're not the investigators, Al."

"This isn't investigating." I closed the book, bringing up a puff of dust. "This is a damn treasure hunt. I don't do treasure hunts."

I started to hand back the journal, but Ollie shook his head and pushed it back to me. "At least try. You can look through any of his other memoirs, maybe find a clue to where he hid it."

"He was your son, why the hell don't you do it?"

He hesitated. "I… can't, Al. Looking through just this one brought back too much already."

I saw the pain on his face and breathed out through my nose, grumbling. "Well… fine. I'll take a look. But no promises."

Ollie smiled, nodding his thanks to say it was enough. Then we heard a gunshot from downstairs.

Glass shattered next, then a scream came from little Stephanie, and metal clatters tumbled after, sounding like a pot falling to the floor.

"Shit." Ollie got to his feet and rushed down the attic.

I was close behind, tucking the journal under

my belt as the others followed hurriedly. It wasn't until we reached the kitchen that we stopped.

"What a nice little home you got here." The pudgy midget tapped off his cigar, the ashes falling to the tiles. He'd taken an apple from the counter and was smacking his lips as he chewed, waving his cane at us. "You got any more chairs, uh? Thought we'd stop by for a family dinner."

I found Rhoda by the stove, stalk still as that combat-looking gal from outside my office had a gun to her head. Glancing left, I saw the tangled, bloody heap of Heph's body in the corner. His head was in another corner.

"Ernie," Ollie growled and looked at the shell shocked faces of the kids at the table. Stephanie's cheeks were drenched. Her father glared back at the dwarf. "In front of my kids?"

He took another bite of the apple, turning to Syrus and Stephanie. He shrugged. "It's educational."

Ollie took a step, but the new gal cocked the gun. "Careful, light rider," she cooed. "We can be civil. For instance, I don't have to blow her fucking brains out in front of her little tykes... unless you make a wrong move. Any of you. Just think of the children, eh?"

Something about Ollie's expression told me it wasn't the children he was worried about. He stole a hard glance behind him, towards the attic we left opened. Then his eyes flicked to me, an order gleaming there. I nodded.

"Syrus," Ollie clipped. "Cephísso. Go with your uncle Al. And do as he says, no questions."

The kids hurriedly pushed out of their chairs to head for me, but Ernie got out his pistol and—

*Bang!*

Syrus took it in the temple and dropped, making his sister scream and duck.

Everyone moved at once.

Ollie lunged for the knife block and grabbed one of the blades, coming at his wife's captor.

The dame took her shot and sunk the bullet in Rhoda's skull just as Ollie heaved the knife at her chest, cutting downward and twisting hard as he pulled out, taking a few soaked intestines with it.

Ernie aimed for him, but Anita slung out her gun faster and *popped!*

He jerked away and was only hit in the shoulder, but as he healed, his skin started changing into a more leathery texture, horns and spines cracking through.

Rhoda and the other gal were just waking up on the floor, and the minute they locked eyes, both grew fangs and their faces paled to marble-white. Black veins spread underneath and into the whites of their eyes until both broads' irises were glinting green and gold. As the rest of them changed into skeletal golems under their now ripped clothes, the things snarled and raged into a demonic brawl on the floor, tearing skin with teeth, ripping out organs with claws, dying and coming back, dying and coming back, all while under the constant, high-pitched wailing of Cephísso under the table by her limp brother.

Ollie and Anita were now taking on the squat goblin, though with kitchen knives instead of claws.

Couldn't they change? Aw, to hell with it, I didn't have time to stand around.

While the golems were all distracted with their fighting, I hustled for the table. Dee followed and picked up the crying girl while I lugged Syrus's body over my shoulder.

We got the hell out of there, Pops ushering us back up the attic. When we made it, we folded the ladder up to us and shut the latch.

"Get the trunk," Pops said.

Dee and I put the kids down to rifle through Orpheus's trunk, taking out all the heavy trinkets and heirlooms, flipping through a few journals to check the last entry dates before tossing the rejects. There were only five books left in there by the end of it, plus the journal I'd tucked away at my belt earlier. When the trunk was light enough, I lifted Syrus's body and laid him out on the lid, then picked the whole thing up by the looped, iron handles. It wasn't easy. A fourteen-year-old wasn't exactly the weight of a toy poodle, but I managed.

Dee picked up Stephanie again, and Pops cracked his knuckles, opening the single window on the wall. "Let's get the hell out of here?"

We didn't pause to agree before falling in line behind him. He stepped out of the way to let me through first. "Jump down."

I craned through the windowsill to stare down at the grass below. It wasn't too far a fall, sure, but it was still the second floor of a building. Immortal or not, it was going to hurt like a bitch.

A piercing shriek gargled below us, clatters banging and more things shattering. It sounded like wild animals fighting over a meal. Another cry cut into my ears, and I glanced back out the window with a deep breath—

Pops shoved me over.

I barely had time to yell when I hit the ground trunk-first. It happened so fast, I slammed into the lid—and teenager's corpse—so hard, I heard a crack from my ribs. Or was that Syrus's spine? Either way, the wind had been knocked out of me and I rolled off, back hitting the soft grass. It took a few painful seconds for the hurt to go away. When it did, I opened my eyes to the overcast sky.

And there, flying with crooked, twisting wings with gnarled feathers, was a golem I didn't recognize. And it was carrying Dee and Cephísso in its disjointed, misshapen arms.

"Pops?" I sat up with a groan as it touched down beside me.

Its head was flat at the brow and curved outward with webbed, splitting horns, snout sleek and bowing into a sharp beak with patched feathers scattered all over the green-tinted skin. When it set down Dee and my niece, its lightning-blue eyes glinted at me. Then with a rupturing, three-toned orchestra accompanying its voice, it said, "Hope you can walk, Al."

I pushed up, testing my legs while stretching my back. "I think so… you look like shit, Pops."

If the thing grinned, it was impossible to tell with that black-tipped beak. But he did, I think, give a low, echoed laugh, facial feathers twitching with the haunting noise.

I shook off a chill and picked up the trunk and

Syrus, who was still dead as an old shoe.

Hefting the two in a breath, I led the way to the street. "Come on, we'll get to my apartment. Ollie knows the way there, and *they* don't."

Dee kept my pace and raised an eyebrow. "You sure about that? We didn't think they knew where this house was."

"How the hell did they find it, anyway?" Pops asked, his demonic physique dissipating back to normal. His wings had already retreated into his back with gross squishing and cracking noises. "Did someone squawk?"

"None of us did, I'm damn sure of that," I muttered. "I don't know anyone else who'd know about it."

I trotted to a stop when we reached the driveway. Someone was sitting on the hood of Ollie's car, swinging her legs as a cascade of orange hair tumbled from one shoulder. Ariel gave a sly grin as she giggled. "Alastor, darling. Fancy seeing you here."

Shit. That clicked quickly enough. I kept a firm grip of the trunk and Syrus. "You ratted us out?"

She waved a hand. "Not at all, dear. We just came to a little arrangement, your old woman and I. My club's getting a second location up in New York, if things turn out well. Zackary, good seeing you again." She winked at Pops.

Dee muttered under her breath to me. "Does she know where your pad is?"

My head shook, not taking my eyes off Ariel while setting down my cargo. I started for my gun, but she already had her pistol aimed at me. "Ah, ah, ah. Let's not try anything too rash? It already looks as if one of the kiddies is down, let's not have two on our hands?" She saw the trunk I'd set down and gestured to it. "What's in there?"

"Stamp collection," I said.

A new voice came from around the car. "I don't remember your brother taking up another hobby."

Dressed in a scarlet coat and veiled bonnet was, of goddamn course, Ma, her ruby heels clacking as she strolled to Ariel. She eyed the trunk at my feet, and the teenager being used as a covering sheet. One of her eyebrows perked. "Looks like Ollie's been popping more little monsters out after all. As for the trunk... what do you think, Aron?"

Her head twisted to the shadowed corner of the house, which I hadn't noticed was occupied until now. The bulky figure under the darkness pushed off the wall and stepped into the light, showing me the biggest fucking giant I had ever lain eyes on.

The body builder had a neck so thick you couldn't wrap three hands around it if you tried. Under a plain T-shirt and denim pants, it looked like he was stuffing a whole suit of armor, bulging shoulders making his head seem tiny, pecs and abs looking bulletproof beneath the over-stretched fabric.

He was a behemoth, so tall he had to duck under a six-foot-high tree limb to make his way to Ma. When his boots crunched the cement, he leaned into the car hood and made the whole damn hunk of metal groan over its tires.

"Looks like a good place to hide a stash of pieces," he said, voice deep and ruptured from his diaphragm.

Ma nodded. "My thoughts exactly, dear. Why don't you go ahead and take that off your younger brother's hands? It looks like he could use some help."

The car groaned again when the boulder removed itself and stalked for me next. I cursed and took out my gun—who cared if Ariel shot hers anyway? I'd walk afterwards—and set it off at his chest.

The bang that rang out made Cephísso squeal in Dee's arms, the bullet piercing through sharp as a whistle. Aron's eyes dimmed for only a second though, and his massive body only swayed for a fraction of that before his attention rekindled mid-step and he started breathing again. Jesus.

Aron shoved me aside with a disinterested push, the motion seeming effortless, but the force blowing the wind out of me when my spine hit the grass.

He kicked Syrus's body off the trunk and opened the lid. His brow knitted. "It's just a bunch of books," he said as he read the metal plate on the lid. "It's some kind of memento to the little fiddler, though."

"Must be old journals," said Ma, tapping a manicured finger to her lips. "Pack them up. They might tell us where he hid the stash."

He shut the lid and hefted the chest over his shoulders like it was a measly house pet, then went to join Ma and Ariel as they started on their way.

But they stopped when Pops called after them. "You're forgetting something, dearest."

A rumble of thunder sounded above, and Ma

twisted on her heels, her scowl softening into a smirk. "Ah. Did I forget to bring an umbrella again?"

"Put the trunk down, Aron," Pops ordered, another grumble sounding overhead, his blue eyes glinting with a small, quick flash.

Aron set down the chest, then cracked his knuckles. "Ball's in your court, Pops. Maybe you'll be more of a challenge this time?"

A rumble came from the overcast clouds overhead, sparks zapping in the night like a tangle of threads. Pops made a shrugging gesture with his head. "Guess we'll find out."

The window beside us shattered, and out fumbled the dwarf-goblin, his wings ripped off and his arm snapped in the wrong direction. It looked to be hanging by a tendon at the shoulder.

While the midget crawled to his feet in an enraged sputter, Heph hopped out of the broken window after him. His head was covered in blood, his skin pink and raw. Had his head grown back?

After Heph came to join us, he noticed Ma and her backup. He grimaced. "Fuck."

That other gal whose name I couldn't remember flew out of there next with mangled wings, her demonic chest leaking with cuts and slash marks that were just starting to heal. Ollie and Anita soon jumped out after her, everyone halting in their tracks to see the crowd in the lawn. Glances were exchanged, curses were muttered, and the storm still rumbled overhead. The rain hadn't started yet.

"Some reunion," Ariel chimed curiously, laying fully on the hood. "Looks like a family matter.

Mind if I sit out for this one?"

Everyone ignored her. The voltage crackled louder, more stringy bolts pulsing like veins as the clouds swirled in a new wind, so strong it nearly blew Ariel off the car hood. The new nimbus looming over us twisted in the pool of electricity, and it wasn't until the rain pattered down that a powerful bolt of lightning crashed down, engulfing Aron's enormous figure to temporarily trap him, that we all jumped.

Things went to shit at this point. Except for Ollie and Anita, the human forms were stripped away to make way for the gargoyles underneath, claws ripping into guts and guns firing anywhere they could hit. Anita and Ollie were the best shots, both packing a pistol in either hand. Ariel, I saw, slipped off the car and snuck out of the warzone quick as a weasel.

Pops was busy trying to take on the big lug while I caught Ma reaching for the chest of journals.

I lunged after it, kicking Ma in the stomach before hefting the trunk by the looped, iron handles. She whirled on me and screamed, skin congealing red and spotted, small horns splitting from her forehead and nose widening. Now she looked more like an ox than a woman, tattered blue-and-green wings cracking out of her shoulder blades and twisting out from her long, fanned tail. Her face was part skin, part fur and part feathers which was, frankly, the scariest fucking thing I ever set eyes on.

But with the way my week had been going, my expectation of "scary" had taken a few leaps. So I dug my heels into the dirt and screamed back at her, my lungs working so hard my vision went red, the terrain splattering with amber and brown. The sensation would have startled me, but seeing this freak bitch's disgusting face and remembering the bullshit she caused my entire, purposeless life, rage boiled up from my stomach and forced my arms to swing the chest at her head. An audible crack came with the motion, and Ma went flying.

That gave me enough time to lug back to Syrus' body, wherever he went. He wasn't where I left him. And I doubted he recovered that quickly, given my own experience.

A stray bullet grazed my cheek, and I yelled. Through the battling gargoyles, heavy shower and chaotic gunfire, though, I found Dee crouched behind the car, Cephísso clinging to her arm and Syrus' corpse at her feet. She must have dragged him out of the warzone. Good girl.

I hobbled over, keeping my head down and making sure the other freaks were nice and distracted with killing each other, and not paying attention to me. When I reached Dee, I nodded for us to get the hell out of here. She didn't object and threw Syrus over her shoulder while we made for the road.

We didn't get too far before a massive, black were-hound bulldozed the car with just its shoulder and launched it in the air, flipping it until it was about to crash right on top of us. We tried to jump out of the way, but Dee was slowed by Syrus' weight and I was fumbling with the chest—

Glass shattered and metal whined when the vehicle landed, catching my legs and lower back with an agonizing crunch. The chest was torn from my hands with the blow, its contents scattering onto the pavement. I screamed and moved to drag myself out from under the wreckage, but the window shards on the ground just bloodied my already stinging palms. With this car's weight, I wasn't going anywhere. I croaked, "Dee?"

Nothing.

The impact left me dazed, my hearing dim and pulsing. Color had seeped out of my vision, except for amber hues splattering everything my eyes drunkenly glided over. A faint whine was ringing in my ears. What the hell was that? It was like an annoying bee buzzing around my head, swelling under the dimness clogging my earholes. There was also a sweet, pungent scent in the air, mixing with the rain.

That tiny wail finally came into full volume when my hearing restored, and I realized it was little Cephísso. "Stephanie," I called, the words slurred. That sweet scent was making me dizzy.

Her crying turned into an undignified blubbering, and I found the chubby girl crushed under the car's mangled hood, only her head and one arm sticking out. She was covered in blood and glass shards shimmered from her brown hair, some sprinkling out as she writhed and wailed in absolute agony.

"Stephanie," I wheezed again, my breath a sliver spewing out of collapsed lungs. "Stephanie, close your eyes. It's all right. It'll stop soon…"

By the looks of her and her fading crying, I knew she was ripe to call it a night. It hurt to hear her sputtering sobs, but then, I had to remind myself she'd wake up again, like Syrus would.

Wouldn't they?

The were-hound who'd thrown the car in the first place crunched its enormous, hook-like claws onto the shattered glass, not giving the shards a second thought as he took his other paw and stomped Cephísso's skull, silencing her incessant wails for good.

I wasn't sure if it was the angle from my place on the ground or the dizzying sweet-scent coming from the car engine, but the hound looked at least a good ten feet tall with a wide girth and foot-long fangs ripping from his perpetually-snarling gums. Its ears were perked and twisted under black fur, eyes gleaming red under the storm as it glared down at me. Then its gaze moved to the toppled trunk of journals, which were soaked and probably ruined now.

The hound went to the soggy books and picked one up, growling. "Well, shit." The sound quivered through my ears, like a siren's screech and beast's rumble melded into one horrific rasp.

The pages sopped out from the binding and slapped next to my outstretched hand. I weakly grasped the soaked paper, which was looking more like plaster mix as the rain poured onto the pavement.

"Ma," the hound called over his shoulder. "Most of the books are ruined."

Though I couldn't see her, I heard her screech. "Save what you can! Just—"

A high pitched cry came from the car engine,

and then I realized what the sweet smell was. Gas. I groaned. "Mother Fu—"

The flames ignited in a cloud of orange, my already red sight blinded as it washed white, heat searing my skin and boiling the blood right out from my veins as my throat ripped a pained scream.

# 9

"What will you do with it all, now?"

I couldn't see the woman. But her voice released a pulsing stream of red streaks in the blackness. Amber and crimson blurs began to form, and I could barely make out the figure in front of me.

The room's details sharpened, beginning as burgundy splotches before clearing up in full blown color. A fire crackled in its hearth by the wall, charred pinewood scenting the air as crisp embers fluttered with the calm smoke. It was some sort of cabin, by the looks of it. There were lamps glaring faint firelight from their glass coverings, flickering silently. Crickets whined outside, so loud it was a wonder you could hear yourself think. But somehow, I tuned them out. It was simple suddenly.

I found myself glancing at the drawn curtains over the windows, suspicion hot in my blood. I was becoming paranoid. All this power, still in my hands after so long... I had to get rid of it. There was talk of my uncle crossing over with grandmother, and Father didn't have to warn me of what they'd do to get their hands on what I had.

It had to go. This plan may not be the best, but I was running out of time. The Alignment would begin tomorrow. Tomorrow... at dawn. Mere hours away.

"Phi?"

My concentration broke, and I turned to Atae. The Iroquois woman was stretched over the bed, sheets strewn about to expose her bare skin as she leered at me under long lashes. Her black hair tumbled over her shoulders and fanned at her muscular back. She was several shades darker than I, with lovely, reddish undertones. She had markings from her previous tribes, hundreds of years' worth of ink. They accentuated every subtle curve of her body in various colors and geometric shapes, but were absent from her swollen belly.

Atae repeated, "What will you do with it all? The Alignment begins tomorrow."

I sighed, pushing aside one of the many wooden crates that surrounded me. The clink of jewels shuffled from inside. "Tomorrow isn't merely the Alignment, my love. I've rallied some of the revolutionists for a special event tomorrow at the harbor. They wish to send the Red Coats a message, and so they shall. But I have other plans for it."

Her brow perked, crawling closer on the bed. "And those plans involve hiding your collection?"

"Indeed they do." I went to meet her, taking a seat before stealing her lips. I held a hand to her belly, smiling to feel a small kick from within. But that smile soon waned when sobriety returned, bringing with it the reminder of what was to come. "We haven't much time. Not much time at all. At dawn…"

"Dawn isn't here yet," she cooed, stroking the hairs at my chest. "Come, your scheming will be of little help this moment. Let us put the night to better use, my love…"

\*\*\*

My head screamed bloody murder when I woke up, feeling like my skin had been seared off.

Because it had been.

I sprang up, ignoring the painful prickles that washed over me. I found my fingers were clenching some soggy paper together, which sopped to the floor when I uncurled my fist.

The journals.

I felt for my beltline and took out the book I'd hidden there. It was tattered and burned near to a crisp.

Looking up, I noticed I was in my own bed, in my apartment. I also saw there were too many damn people. Everyone was startled when I gasped alive, save for the charred corpses of Syrus and poor little Cephísso. They looked like they were healing still.

"What happened?" I croaked, my throat dry.

There was a strained silence among them, most glancing away. Ollie was the only one to answer. "They took the journals. And they torched my house. And none of us have any pieces now."

I pursed my lips, not sure what comforting thing I could say. I'd apparently been a useless corpse during the last bit of it. The most I could come up with was. "I'm sorry."

Ollie sighed hard, Rhoda taking his arm to console him. "We don't have much time left," he said. "The Alignment starts at dawn."

"Dawn?" I echoed. That sounded familiar… like

my dream.

The dream!

"Ollie," I blurted, my memory rearing its wonderful, ugly head. "What year was the last Alignment?"

Ollie blinked at me, glancing at Pops and shrugged. "17-something."

"'73," said Dee on the other side of the bed.

Anita looked surprised. "73? It's early this time?"

I tucked the burnt journal back in my beltline and pushed off the bed, getting my coat—only to realize I was still wearing it. But it was scorched and in pieces, covered in blood and soot... Aw, to hell with it. I kept it on, grabbing a pistol from the desk-drawer in the corner. My last gun had apparently been taken off my person while I was dead. Newly armed and loaded, I went to the door and threw it open.

Heph and Rhoda stayed behind to watch after the kids while the others followed me down the iron stairwell to the street. Dee was the first to question, "Where are you going?"

"To the harbor," I said, itching for a smoke, but knew there wasn't time. But boy could I use one.

Ollie sounded puzzled. "Why?"

"Let's just say our forefathers weren't only dumping bags of dried up leaves down there."

\*\*\*

When we reached the docks of the Botson harbor, Ollie snagged my shoulder to stop me from running off. "Are you sure it's here?" he asked.

I shrugged. "That's what I… uh, your son was yapping about."

His brow knitted. "Did you read that in the journals?"

"Not exactly." I slipped out the tattered journal and looked it over. "I sort of lived it. Or, saw it, maybe. I don't know. Either way, this is where he said he'd put it. We have to find a way to fish them out of the bottom of these docks."

Anita scoffed. "How in hell are we going to do that?"

"And even if we found a way to haul them up," Pops muttered. "The harbor's huge. There's no telling the exact spot they were dumped, not to mention if they were moved around from the tides over the last 200 years."

I scanned the docks, watching the anchored ships lull in the glassy waves. "Doesn't matter," I said. "Because I think I know a way to find out. But we need a boat."

"No cash," grunted Ollie.

"Then we'll hitch one." My steps clunked over the boardwalk as I moved to the line of abandoned motorboats, examining each one. Luckily, it was the wee hours of the morning, so there was no one here to stop us. After checking a good dozen vessels, only one had the keys conveniently hidden under the bench.

"Guess this will have to do," I said, grimacing at the tiny thing, but knowing our straws were getting shorter by the minute, so I damn well better count my blessings.

I ushered everyone in and untied the ropes holding the pitiful boat down, then pushed off and ripped on the motor. When we were a fair distance away, and I was sure Ma and her crew weren't anywhere near us, I stopped the boat and peeled open the burnt journal. I had no idea if this would work on demand, but now was as good a time as any to find out.

I inhaled sharply, shutting my eyes and pressed my fingers against the pages.

I counted the seconds down, waiting to see those amber streaks again… But nothing happened.

I peeked an eye open and turned a few pages, trying to jumpstart whatever had happened in my 'sleep'… Oh.

"Shit." I shut the book, slipping out my gun.

Dee looked confused beside me. "What?"

I blew out a breath and cocked the gun, setting it at my temple. "For the love of God, make sure I don't drop the book."

*Bang!*

\*\*\*

The splatters of amber came rushing in. They weren't fully formed yet, but they washed over the black nothingness like a masterful painting.

I heard a voice then. Well, not necessarily a voice, but muffled sobs.

The blurs sharpened soon, showing me in a small, disheveled room, thin robes and dirt all over the floor. There wasn't a bed, but a pile of scratchy hay in the center.

There was a man wearing what looked like nothing more than a sheet by the door, downing a flask of...

Oh, only the Gods knew what poison was in there tonight.

When he was finished with the red drink that stained his robes, he peered into the flask with one eye winked and the other bulging longingly, as if searching for even a drop left inside. When he found none, his throat ripped forth an enraged snarl, and he threw the flask against the wall, shattering it and forcing another scream from me.

Realizing I'd drawn attention to myself, I clasped my hands round my lips to stifle the cries, huddling farther in the corner, tears dripping on my knees. My heart raced in my ears, drowning my mind's command to run. *Run.* Far away from here, like Mother had done, away from the monster, the beast.

"Are you listening to me, girl?" he roared in Greek, slamming a fist against the side table. The bowl that had been set there clattered in his wake. "I know what you've done. Don't try to deny you took what you right well know was mine."

He came and grabbed my hair, ripping upward to force me to my feet.

"I-I took nothing!" I yelped, the pain stinging my scalp. "Nothing...!"

"Damned little snake, you." He shoved my face against the window, the glass cracking along with my nose as I sank back to the floor. "It was my wine, paid with my money."

"I only t-took a sip. Just a sip, it wasn't...!"

His anger grew and he hefted the iron candlestick, lashing it down.

"How—" he said, striking my jaw. "-can I afford—" My brow throbbed at the second hit. "-a damned—" My lip split. "-*thief?*" He hit my temple, sending me to the dirt.

By the end of it, I could barely breathe, let alone move. He would have continued, if the drink hadn't overtaken him and coaxed him to slumber on the hay. I crawled over the ground, my blood streaking the dirt and ruining what was left of my black robe, and pulled myself up at the table. The Gods had mercy, for my legs were merely bruised, unlike my wrist. It had been twisted and bent in the wrong angle, the pain incredible.

Through the blood dripping in my eye, I glared at the man slumbering on the hay. Damn him. Damn him, *damn him*. "May you choke on your precious wine," I spat, then left this place forever.

***

This time, waking up wasn't so hard. It was more of a rush now, the wind jamming its way into my lungs and prying open my eyes in a sharp gasp.

I was on the boat's floor, staring up at the stars. The three brightest, I noticed, were nearly in a straight line.

When I started coughing, Ollie and Anita peered down at me.

"That didn't take as long, at least," Anita muttered.

"He's building a tolerance," agreed Ollie.

I sat up, rubbing my eyes. "Tolerance or not, it still hurts like no tomorrow."

"So," Pops said from the helm. He set his elbows on the wheel. "Mind telling us why you bothered?"

"Yeah." Dee glowered from the ledge, dipping a hand in the water to wash my blood off her face. "Better have been worth it. Warn me next time you decide to fall my way, at least."

I stared at her, pointing. "Was that you?"

She glared back. "Was what me?"

"The girl... Never mind." I searched the boat for the journal, finding it at my feet and picked it up with a click of my tongue. "It didn't show me what I wanted."

"What does that mean?" Asked Ollie.

"Every time I die, I see something. Scenes or whatever. I was hoping to see the exact spot Orpheus dumped his stash, but..."

"—Ah," a new voice piped up to my left. "Should have guessed it'd be you lot."

My head snapped to the guy who'd risen from the water to prop his elbows on the boat. He was grinning wildly, like he'd just heard a joke.

"Who the hell are you?" I asked, getting to my feet.

The intruder shrugged, still halfway in the water. "The wise guy whose boat you stole to get here," he said and shot a wink at Dee. "How's it hanging, sweetheart? Like the bob, it suits you."

Dee set her hands at her sides. "Of course you'd be in the area, Pedro."

"I go by Paul these days."

"Paul," she drawled, as if testing it out. "I like it. Let me guess: you're hunting for the stash, too?"

"Hunting for it?" he laughed, his annoying grin widening. "Honey, you're in my domain, here. The sea is my mistress, my backyard, yadda, yadda, whatever you want to call it. I found that beautiful stash of pieces a few decades ago."

Ollie pushed Dee aside. "Paul, we need some pieces. We're not asking for all of them, just enough for the lot of us, and my kids."

Paul rubbed a hand under his nose in a sniff. "What happened to yours? The old hag got her mitts on 'em?"

"More like sicked her dog on us," Anita said.

Paul's expression soured. "Sounds like a heap of trouble. One that I personally don't want to get involved with, 'specially so close to Alignment."

"You won't have to be involved," Ollie assured. "Just give us enough pieces to survive this round."

"And if one of you decides to tell the hag and her goons?"

Ollie's glare darkened. "You know damn well that stash belonged to my son. The last thing we want is for his killer to get his hands on it himself. We won't say squat to our Ma. In fact, we're going to kill her and her little favorites this round."

He cocked an eyebrow. "Didn't you try that last time? Didn't go so well, last I remember."

"Pedro," Ollie said, then amended. "Paul. Please."

Paul took a long time to consider. But after a while, he heaved himself out of the water and took the helm from Pops. "All right, sure. But I ain't doing this for you, you know. Phi was a good friend. I'd love to see the bastard who killed him get what's coming to him. Hold onto your purses, fellas."

He slammed the boat into full speed as we skipped over the waves in a rush of wind.

# 10

Paul steered us off the main docks toward the bank of Lovell Island.

Fort Standish looked active tonight, the two lighthouses sweeping their beams from east to west, orange lamplight glowing from the camp and casting shadows of the crawling troops and military vehicles transporting them around the base. The gun batteries loomed in the distance behind them.

"You hid the stash over here?" asked Ollie over the boat motor, looking at Paul uncertainly. "Aren't you worried the Coast Guard will find it?"

Paul gave a nervous laugh from the helm, scratching under his nose. "Actually, uh, they already did."

"What?" I clipped next to Ollie. "When the hell did that happen?"

"Some years ago," he coughed, sounding embarrassed. "I kept it all down there, figuring no one would come looking for it, but boy was I not expecting those Germans to make underwater ships. I found that hunk of metal blown to smithereens next to the stash. It was a miracle the crate didn't get hit by the blast, but then our boys over here came snooping and found the pieces."

Anita sounded incredulous. "And they what, just kept it on the fort without trying to spend it?"

"If they did, they wouldn't get any cash out of

it. It's an unknown gem here, the jewelers would just think they're fakes. Either way, that's where it is, last I checked."

"You're sure?" Dee and Pops asked, disbelieving.

Paul nodded. "Should be there. Just have to get past all the artillery. Dying ain't really a problem for us, least not until sun-up, but getting caught and locked up in a concrete cell for God knows how long is."

I smeared a hand over my face, wiping off the coarse sea water. "So, what's the plan? Ram the boat up there and hope they don't start shooting?"

He shrugged. "Figured we could try for the northern tip. It's the most hidden from the rest of… aw, hell."

Other motors sounded ahead of us, and two larger boats came from either side to block us, forcing Paul to cut off the engine. One of the boats had a big, blinding light aimed right at us, so bright I had to shield a hand over my watering eyes.

A voice fuzzed from a megaphone. "You're trespassing on U.S. military property. Either state your purpose or turn around before we blow you sky high."

Anita, behind me, grumbled something under her breath and fished into her coat pocket. She pulled out a badge and raised it over her head, standing up. "Agent Anita Déus. CIA. I'm here with my team, and our purpose is confidential. Blow us sky high, and the agency brings more to level this fort and anyone in it. Capeesh?"

Silence from the megaphone, but there were

whispers on both boats. Anita put her badge away and set a hand on her hip. "Now, if you don't mind, I'd like to speak with your Chief Petty Officer."

The megaphone fuzzed on again, the voice more hesitant now. "R… right away, Agent Déus. Let us escort your vessel."

One led the way to the island's docks while the other trailed behind us, and I gawked at her as we sputtered along. "Are you actually…?"

"Yeah." She said. "What better way to hide and blend in than to take on an investigative job that looks for these things? I hide evidence, and they don't think twice about me."

I grinned. "Don't suppose I can call on you for connections in future cases? You know. Family and all."

She snorted. "Opportunist, you are."

In about ten minutes we reached the docks and tied up the boat, the men from the Guard helping us out before turning on their transceivers and explaining to, I guessed, the CPO that we wanted to meet with him. After a minute, the grunt nodded and waved for us to follow him through the camp.

There had to be at least 300 troops on the island. The dirt roads had thick tire tracks going in every direction alongside footprints and snuffed cigarette butts. The sea breeze came in and rustled the small thickets of trees scattered around the base, smoke coming from one of the brick building's chimney. Judging from the smell of cooked pork and beans, I figured that was the mess hall.

Our group paused to let a vehicle through, the engine sputtering and growling as it left a dark haze from its exhaust pipe. The spiced scent made me want a smoke, so I took out a box of Lucky's from my pocket and lit one up. Ollie slipped one out of the box before I could put it away and asked Dee for a light, who complied while taking a smoke for herself from my box, followed by Pops, and lastly by Anita. By the time those vultures were done snatching my smokes, there was only one left in there. I scowled, jerking it away when Paul tried to swipe it up. Like hell I was going to let this shmuck get the last one I might ever have. Damned scavengers.

We were led into one of the quarters, the floorboards creaking under our feet, and were taken to a small office down the hall. The door was opened when we went in. The CPO was sitting behind his desk waiting for us, and told the grunts to shut the door and leave. They saluted and high tailed it out of there.

There were only two chairs on our side of the desk, and Dee was the only one to take the liberty. The rest of us stood where we were as Anita crossed her arms.

"You in charge here?" she asked.

"I am." The chief's tone leaked with suspicion. "Want to explain what the CIA is doing in my base? And covered in old blood stains, no less?"

Anita's business-like demeanor didn't waver. "It's come to our attention that a suspicious package may have been taken here."

His brow furrowed. "Suspicious package?"

"There've been rumors of a crate being found some years ago, when one of the German boats was found destroyed by one of your mines. Inside the crate was said to be strange… crystals. Ones that no jewelers recognize and can put a price tag on."

The chief's complexion blanched. "Haven't heard anything like that around here. Guess your Intel is faulty. Maybe check the other beacons."

Anita's fingers drummed over her arm, thoughtful. Then she drew in a breath from her cigarette and blew the smoke in his face, pressing a hand on the desk. "Let me make this clear. My team and I are going to turn this shithole inside out whether you like it or not. If we find what we're looking for, and find out you knew it was here, then I can't guarantee you'll keep your rank at this fort. Or any rank, anywhere. Try and kill us, and more will come in our place to find out what happened to us, and you'll be lucky if you leave without bullet holes. Get me?"

He swallowed.

"Now," she said and took another puff, a soft *puft* sounding when she slid it from her lips and pronounced each syllable slowly, smoke curling with each breath. "I'm going to ask again. Are there any foreign crystals on this island?"

He squirmed in his seat, the chair creaking under his weight. He couldn't seem to find a comfortable position. After a minute of uncertain coughs, he exhaled. "I… might've heard something along those lines. At the lighthouse."

"Good." She smiled, straightening. "Then you won't mind taking us there?"

He glowered, probably sending mental daggers her way, but went to the transceiver at his desk and told an officer to bring him a truck. Then he pushed out of his chair and went to open the door, telling us to follow him outside.

But before we made it out, we heard shouts from the camp. Then they congealed into screams.

"What the hell?" I hurried out first, trying to get a peek of what the hollering men were looking at. It didn't take long to find it. Stepping out of the thicket of trees was a giant, demonic hound, red eyes glinting in the dark. It stomped down a foot, crunching the soft dirt underneath, jagged teeth barred.

"What a lovely party." Ma's voice came from behind the doggish gargoyle, the woman herself stepping next to him. "And I hear the goody bags are more than generous."

An earsplitting shriek burst behind me, making me spin. Perched on the quarters' stone overhanging was another creature, feminine this time, with twisted, brown wings sporting black spots on the feathers. The thing's eyes were huge and unblinking. They didn't move in their sockets, but her head craned here and there with haunting silence, the only sound coming from her beaked muzzle, which was grating and loud and damn near made me want to rip off my ears.

The cry blew back the gaping troops and made most of them tremble, either leaping back a good yard, dropping their rifles, or falling on their asses. I could have sworn I smelled piss from the chief.

"How the hell did you find us?" asked Ollie, taking out a gun that was strapped to his belt.

Anita was doing the same, and I even saw Dee

and Pops pull out their own firearms. Obviously, I took out mine, too.

Ma held up a beat up old journal, tapping a finger over the spine. "We only had to go through a few of these to notice a little mention of the harbor. And wouldn't you know, when we went down to check it out, there was this little boat out on the water, heading to this island. We thought it was worth a look."

I wasn't surprised when that old midget, Ernie, came waddling up next to her, taking a swig from a flask. "Thanks, by the way," he said, smacking his lips and screwing on the cap. "Would've been a longshot to find it otherwise."

My view shifted to the sky. It was getting brighter towards the east. If we waited any longer, it'd be sunrise before we even got to the lighthouse. And when that happened, the only ones who couldn't die would be them. The rest of us would be slaughtered.

I glanced to my right. That truck the chief asked for was parked a few yards away, engine sputtering with life. I took in a slow breath, hissing to Dee next to me. "Sorry."

She frowned. "For what—"

I whipped my gun at the owl girl above the doorway and shot it right in the head. The minute she dropped at our feet, I shoved Dee towards the truck and shouted. "Get in!"

She leapt over the side of the open back and I jumped in after, barking at the driver to get the fuck out. He almost face planted he got his ass out of there so quick, and I took his seat, slammed the gear in drive and kicked that pedal to the floor. The engine roared and plumed with exhaust as we sped off.

# 11

I twisted back, trying to see what Dee and I were leaving behind.

It looked like god damn Armageddon over there. Ollie and Anita were taking on Aron, Pops had changed and was hacking away at Ma, Paul took on a fishy, demon form and was going against the owl bitch who recovered from being shot.

"Al!" Dee barked, pointing ahead. "Tree!"

My head snapped forward, and I swerved ungracefully around the tree, getting back on track. Right. Focus on driving.

All I could hear behind me now were the screams of the terrified troops in the distance, the hellish, over-toned snarls of the gargoyles, gunshots exploding from every direction, and pained wails from, I guessed, the unlucky collateral damages.

It all faded when we reached the two lighthouses, only the soft *pops* and rattling gunfire could be heard now.

I cut the engine and hopped out, Dee fumbling after me as I started for the first lighthouse on the boardwalk. Luckily, the next one was right down the ways beside it. But we had to cross over a thicket of trees to get to either.

"I'll take the first one," I told her, twigs crunching under my shoes. "You look in the second."

She pushed a branch out of her way. "It'd better be here, or I swear to god I'm torching the place."

A new twig snapped behind us, making us freeze. We spun, but relaxed. It was just a grunt with a rifle. The poor guy was shaking as he aimed for Dee.

Dee sighed and grabbed the barrel. The skin melted from her face, hair a quivering black fire as her boney jaw clicked and clacked a fiery order. "Scram."

A wet stain trailed down his pant leg, his grip loosening on the rifle. Dee yanked it out of his hand, shoving him aside. He didn't stay more than two seconds before getting the hell out of there.

Her skull went back to normal, skin and eyes returning. Her hair, though, was still scorched and wavering down to her chin. "Here, big cat." She tossed me the rifle. "Thought you'd like a bigger gun."

"Damn right I would." My grin was mischievous.

We stepped out of the thicket. But our feet only crunched the dirt when a winged shadow hurtled over our heads and touched down to block our way. It was a clumsy landing, its tangled wings fumbling on the dirt. But she quickly recovered her footing and staggered to her taloned feet.

A red glint came from a stick that was speared through the owl's tied up bun. It was Dee's cigarette holder, the gem glittering at the centerpiece.

"I call this one." Dee's skin melted off again, stepping up front. The skeleton crouched, throat clicking and bones rattling. "Go find the stash."

"You sure about this?" I asked, tightening my hold of the rifle and alternating gazes at the she-demons.

"Oh yeah." Her boney brow, god knows how, slid down a grinding notch and furrowed over the empty eye sockets. She was staring at the smoking stick in the owl woman's hair. "She and I are just going to have a little *chat*."

The last part was screamed, black fire blazing from her hands and hair, blue embers sparking from her mouth as she grew foot-long boney claws and lunged for the owl.

The owl's talons stretched from her own fingers and deflected Dee's swipe, bringing them to a tree trunk and scratching the bark right by my head. I ducked under their entangled arms, sprinting to the boardwalk as their shrieks and crackles flared behind.

I finally made it to the boardwalk, throwing open the first lighthouse's door and hustling up the tower. I got to the revolving light up top, scanning the small space. But there was nothing here. No crate full of crystals, nothing hidden in a false wall or floor… it was empty. The stash, if it was here at all, must have been in the other tower.

Griping my rifle, I chewed on a curse and started back down the spiraling stairs.

The metal door was torn from its hinges with a rupturing tremor. Then, god damn it, Aron trudged inside. The giant hound had ripped the thing off by just slamming into it.

"Shit." I cocked my rifle—then blasted his head open.

The lug only staggered a fraction before the wound sealed and he was climbing after me again. "Shit, shit, shit."

I ran back up, stopping at the glass room with the revolving light. There was a small, railed terrace that circled the glass cylinder. I found the panel with a latch and opened it, stepping out and gripped the rail. The tall grass under the boardwalk hushed in the breeze, the smell of gunpowder fogging the air, rifle shots still exploding by the camp in the distance. Puffing, I saw the sky was brightening, the first rays of the sun spewing over the sea's horizon. Sunrise. We're almost out of time.

Aron's hulky footfalls pounded against the steps, seeming slow compared to my pulse, sweat dripping into my eye. I didn't care to squint, though. There wasn't time. No time. No time...

The other tower was too far for me to make it before sunrise. Even if the stash was in there, it would take me too long to jump down, run the boardwalk, get up the stairs and grab it before Aron ripped my appendages off. In another minute, the next time I died would be the last.

Aron came snarling, red eyes spotting me on the other side of the glass. I lunged away when he slammed his doggish head on the glass, making it shatter. Shards rained down the length of the tower and pattered over the boards. The hound clambered toward me.

"Well," I panted, "now or never."

I flung myself over the rail.

I gagged to a stop when the dog caught me by the neck, my legs flailing under me and hitting the tower wall on the other side of the rail. "Where're you going, little fish?" he laughed, multi-toned voice grating my eardrums.

He smashed my face through a glass panel, tossing me inside so fast, I hit the panel across from it and broke through. By the time my head stopped spinning, I found myself craned over the rail by the stomach, temples throbbing, neck cracking painfully and chunks of sharp glass wedged in my shoulder. There was blood dripping down my arm. I reached a hand to my head, groaning, and found out I could barely hear anything. My ears were ringing. I fumbled to the walkway, spitting up blood as I thunked my head against a pole.

Most of the sun had risen above the watery horizon now.

But I wasn't dead yet.

That thought was crushed along with my windpipe. Aron had crouched to meet my eyelevel. The gargoyle sounded bored. "How about we watch the sunrise together, little brother?"

I clutched a bloody hand over his arm, wheezing...

But I blinked. My vision had unfocused, Aron covered in red static. The crimson splotches spread past his figure, painting the whole of my sight until I couldn't see anything but red.

Then, sluggishly, the hues changed in undefined splotches, which soon sharpened back into focus. Aron was still here, but he was a ways away and in a field, not strangling me on a lighthouse. The others surrounded us, Ollie and Anita to my right, Pops and Dee to my left...

\*\*\*

Dawn had long past come. But it hadn't been long since I found my wife naked and dumped in the harbor. Her neck was snapped the wrong way. Her groin had been torn asunder… and she hadn't woken. She'd lost her piece.

Aron's canine ears curled back, barking. "So, nephew? Where have you hidden that bounty?"

My breaths were ragged, tears dried and crusted on my cheeks. He hadn't even given Atae a second thought. Already banished from mind. The rage spilled from my lips like molten steel. "You'll find your bounty when I send you to hell."

Fury possessed my arms, mounting my violin over a shoulder and flung the bow over the strings. The notes came as a haze, scratching and wailing and flurrying in a storm of hate, tears spilling as the fire consumed that infernal pit burdening my chest, my feet driving forward, venom surging through my veins and bubbling forth a knot of anguish, the tempest spewing and casting a maelstrom of screams—

\*\*\*

Back on the lighthouse under Aron's grip, the painful burn of vengeance still flared, the last scream still pushing out of my throat as the fire pumped through my muscles, shoving out my bones until they cracked out of place, rearranging themselves as my jaw unhinged and shifted, my cheekbones and brow sinking with agonizing cricks and grotesque crunches.

My nails grew into six inch claws, I felt my teeth sharpen and bow, then caught in the gale of fury, I shoved my fingers point first into Aron's chest, feeling the soft tissue of his heart around my nails. The dog's red eyes bulged at me, whispering. "Orpheus...?"

A glint came from a studded gem pierced to the hound's ear. He had a second one on the other ear. My glare bore into his, voice oscillating in a perfectly pitched, multi-toned chord of blissful music as words that weren't mine came from my lips. "I'd love to watch the sunrise with you, dearest uncle."

I ripped my hand out of his chest and tore out his earrings. He gave a pained howl and stumbled into the glass room, the sunlight beaming over the terrain as the hound lost his bulky form, fading back to human, and grew stiff over the broken lamp in the center.

I held both pieces in either hand, the things glinting with their own, radiant light. I glanced at the body in the room. His wounds weren't healing. My eyes moved to the sky, squinting at the sunlight. Despite the glare, I could still see the three stars to its left. They were in line.

Heat permeated from the pieces, leaking into my palms and raged through my veins until I thought my eyes would melt. It was painful, but intoxicating. I started laughing.

Footsteps clunked on the boardwalk below, making me crane down to see the others had rushed over. Dee had gotten her smoking stick back, but Ollie and Anita still looked empty handed. Pops wasn't here, as far as I could tell. Neither was Paul.

The three of them drew back when finding me. For the first time, I finally got to see Ollie's other… form. In the sunlight, his eyes were a bright gold, along with the twisting wings and mangled feathers that shone in the beautiful rays.

His contorted voice faltered as he peered up at me. "Orpheus…?"

I glanced at a glass panel behind me, catching my reflection in the cracked surface. I didn't look like me. I'd also taken on a demonic form, but it didn't *feel* like my own. It was someone else's.

I flinched when my reflection waved at me without me moving an inch, and a soft voice hissed in my ear.

*Thank you…*

The form faded along with the voice. My bones cracked back to my usual physique. I stared at me again. No gargoyle attached. With fatigue weighing down my shoulders and my thoughts shot to hell, I made my way down the tower steps, leaving Aron's body where it was. When I headed out to the boardwalk, Ollie was staring at me like he'd seen a ghost.

"What?" I asked.

He was still staring, his human form returning. "Did you kill Aron?"

My gaze shifted up, then back down. "Yeah." I felt just as surprised as he looked.

"How?"

I shrugged. "I… bled on him."

He frowned, and I shook my head, getting out my last smoke and lighting it. "Turns out, I don't need to shoot myself to see things. Bleeding works fine. I'll try and stick with that."

Dee shoved past him and looked me up and down. "And why did you look like Orpheus just now?"

Another shrug. "I just borrowed the look, I guess. He wanted me to do him a favor."

They all didn't seem to get it, still trying to wrap their heads around it. Made sense to me. Kind of.

I took a hit from the smoke and gestured to Ollie. "Are you stuck as a mortal now or what?"

Ollie's amber eyes rekindled with awareness, and he laughed. "I got Athena's piece when Dee took her down. Even if I didn't, though, the Alignment lasts all day, till sunrise tomorrow. Anita's vulnerable now, but as long as she gets a piece by then, she's good. Same with Rhoda and the kids. I'll get them their pieces in time."

I grunted. "Let's get on with it, then. It wasn't in that tower, so I figure it's in the next one."

Ollie nodded and led the charge ahead. I trailed behind, stuffing my hands in my pockets... but stopped. These weren't technically lighthouses, were they? They looked too short for it. More likely, they were range lights. If they thought the stash was valuable, why would they put something in such unsecure structures that could easily flood in a storm? My guess was, they wouldn't. And I also didn't trust the petty officer to give us the true location, but it was safe to assume he'd give us a false lead to make us think they really didn't have it. It seemed likely enough. But if I were to hide precious gems in a small island like this and didn't want the CIA to find it, where would I put it?

I looked out to the horizon. In the distance, almost right between these two range lights was a lookout tower. It was a large slab of rectangle, looking heavily fortified. It also looked like a good place to hide a stash of gems you didn't want to be found.

"Wait," I called, making Ollie turn back when I pointed to the tower. "Why don't we pay that little pad a visit?"

We made our way over, climbing the steps inside without any problems. It looked like the troops, if they'd been in here, had hurried out to help at the camp earlier. Or just ran. Either way, they weren't here anymore. It took an hour of snooping around the place before finding a tiny, locked up box in a hole in the wall. It had been covered with a loose stone to hide it. Props to them, too, I barely saw the imperfection. But saw it, I did.

When I opened the box, I found a small collection of the red gems. Had to admit, the pile was smaller than I expected. The whole thing was about the size of a fist. There couldn't have been only that much in those dozen crates Orpheus had stacked up in his house back then.

The gems were beautiful, though. They were like uncut opals, amber glitter sparkling from inside the red stones and giving off their own light.

I tossed in the studded earrings I took from Aron and palmed a bigger, more oval looking one. "Is this it?"

"There has to be more," Dee protested, looking at the box from over my shoulder. "Keep looking."

We did. We looked all around the tower, back near the boardwalk, in both range lights, even walked all the way to the gun batteries and the barracks, but this one box was all there was. Orpheus must have sent the other pieces somewhere else. I guess it made sense: why put all your eggs in one basket?

Still. I had a bad feeling. If that stash was split up and sent off to who knows how many places, then who all found it during this Alignment? How many new immortals would come out of this? And what godforsaken talents would they have, and what were the odds we wouldn't run into them? Jesus, the world could be crawling with fuckers like Aron, and that bastard at least did what Ma said and stayed out of sight from the public.

I rubbed my forehead, groaning. Part of me didn't want to keep immortality. A bigger part was all for it, hell yeah, but bigger than that was wanting to make sure we didn't blow ourselves up in the next century.

We found Pops back at camp, outside the quarters with Paul. The boys from the coast guard were either dead or had hightailed it out of here already, so far as I could see. Pops had apparently taken Ma's piece for himself. She was left mortal, cuffed and shoved to the dirt, glaring up at me. Ernie had disappeared. He probably hitched one of the boats and skedaddled when things got sticky, the little worm.

I loomed over Ma, cocking an eyebrow. "You

killable now?"

"Fuck you," she spat, face caked in dirt and blood painting her lip.

"Your dog's dead now, by the way," I informed with a sniff. "Same with the owl girl... I think Ollie called her Athena?"

Her expression cracked, looking surprisingly destitute. "My babies...? What have you done...?"

She started weeping now. Dee bent to pet a group of crows that had flown over and landed by her feet, looking up at me and asked. "What do we do with her?"

I drew in a puff from my smoke, flicking off the ash and hummed. "Well, I was originally going to shoot her brains out, but I think I've got something better in mind."

# 12

"We, the jury, find the defendant guilty of all charges."

The judge slammed his gavel, and I watched as Ma was hauled out of the court by the coppers. Dee was sitting next to me, having given her testimony as witness to Darryl Heler's murder, and rose when I stretched up, shuffling out of the benches.

*This* was worse than death, I figured. Having lost both her favorites, along with her immortality, now she got to spend the rest of her shortened life in a cellblock. Or maybe even in a Psych ward, if I was lucky. Pure poetry, that was.

Captain Hunter came to slap my back. "Damn good work, Al. And thank you, Miss Dee, for warming up to us."

She smiled, shooting me a fixed glare. "I'm just glad she's getting what she deserves, Earl."

When we left the courthouse and started down the dark street, Dee's voice dropped to a mutter. "Any sign of Ariel?"

"Nah," I said, "My guess is she left town."

I tipped my hat to the two crows that were perched on a road sign, their mangy feathers giving off an orange sheen under the streetlamp. One of them fluttered its wings and stretched its neck down to me, an old, dried up Lucky in its beak.

I grimaced, but forced a grin, taking the smoke.

"Thanks, pal."

The crow cawed, as if proud of itself, and flew off. Once it was gone, I stuffed the disgusting smoke in my coat pocket. The winged rats and I were on good terms, sure, but there was no telling how many gull livers those beaks have munched on. Still, it was a nice gesture. I didn't want to hurt the little goblin's feelings.

Pops had left earlier in the week. He went back to Jersey empty-handed save for one gem. He'd left the stash with Paul and us, though reluctantly. He realized he'd never get those pieces to his gang before sunrise, since we found it so late. So, he bit the bullet on that one. He seemed sore about it, but when I reminded him Ma was at least taken care of, he cheered up and left on a good note.

But speaking of fathers…

I glanced at Dee with a narrow eye. "Say, can I ask you something?"

She was busy shoving a cigarette in her holder. "You can ask me anything, big cat."

"In light of my talent for family feuds and carrying out revenge…"

She lit the end with her enflamed finger, taking a puff. "Mm-hmm?"

"I might have caught a glimpse of what your old man was like."

Her clicking heels went silent. "What? When?"

"On the boat, when you caught me after I shot myself. And as a side note, if I try that again, stop me."

"I might not want to," she growled, looking ripe to bring out little Miss Bones. "I've never told anyone about my father. If you say anything to the others—"

"I won't," I said. "I just want to know what happened. After you left home, I mean. I only saw you walk out."

She clicked her tongue and took a hit from her smoking stick, tapping out the ashes. "You really want to know?"

I waited for her to breathe the smoke out her nose. Then she said, "I took a candelabra from the kitchen and chucked it at the hay where he was sleeping. Burned the place to the ground, with him in it. Then I buried his burnt corpse in an empty grave he himself dug the night before and left him for the crows to peck out what was left of his organs."

As gruesome as it was, I snorted a laugh. "Of course you did. Well, the bastard had it coming. And you wonder why fire's part of your talent?"

She shrugged, sighing. "I suppose they say the past follows us."

"No kidding." I said. "What did you get from helping us, anyway? You said Ollie was going to give you something."

The new subject made her face brighten. "Oh. That. Yeah, he and Rhoda gave me… advice."

"On?"

She blew more smoke, waving the stick dismissively. "How to have a kid."

I spun on her, staring. "That's what you wanted to know?"

"It's not simple for us, you know," she snapped. "Apparently, an immortal can only mate with another immortal to get one. And to top it off, it looks like I *also* need to go nine months without getting killed, or even changing form. Nine! That's god damn ridiculous."

"Why do you want a kid?"

She circled a wistful hand in the air, smoke trailing from the cigarette. "Oh, I don't know. It's been a few thousand years, and everyone else seems to like it... besides, just think: Death giving life? Ha!"

"Ha, ha, ha," I muttered. "A god damn comedian, this one..."

She winked, tossing her head back. "What do you say, big cat? Interested?"

I grimaced. "I don't want kids."

"Oh, I just need an immortal to make it, you won't have to do any parenting. I'd take care of it myself."

"Christ Almighty, in that case, I might just do it to get custody rights." I shook my head and walked on. "That kid won't last a day in your care when he pops out."

She almost snapped back at me, but paused, catching up to my pace. "So you'll do it?"

I scowled, reaching my office door and driving the key in the lock. "We'll... see." I pulled open the door, nodding for her to come in. "Maybe if you're a good enough secretary first."

She walked through, stiffening to see the potbellied dwarf inside was shoving the new desk into place on the carpet. "Ernie?" Her brow furrowed at me. "What the hell's he doing in here?"

"Looks like he's doing what I asked," I said,

nodding to the short stack. "Thanks, Ern. You cleaned this place up nice."

The dwarf straightened and brushed himself off, smiling. "Thanks, Boss. Got the desk, just like you asked."

"That you did."

Dee drummed her fingers over an arm as if waiting for an explanation. I shrugged. "He showed up at my office and asked to work for me."

"Now that Ma's locked up," Ernie said and took off his bowler hat, looking solemn as he turned it in his fingers. "I got nowhere to go. And I wasn't the one who torched Ollie's place, anyways."

"You were with the people who did," noted Dee. "And you shot Syrus."

Ernie threw up his hands. "I knew the kid'd get back up! So did you, when I clocked you, toots, but sounds like you already forgot about it. Ehhhh, look, Hades. I know I'm asking too much already, but, uh… I'll try and make up for it. Ma left some money up in New York, I figure I can pull that out and get Ollie a new pad, and even pitch myself in some place down here, but… I don't know what to do, now. We had a plan with Ma, and now Ma's shut up in jail."

"So you came here?" muttered Dee.

"Well I thought, you know, why not stick with Al, huh?" He waddled over to punch my arm. He could only reach my elbow. "Get to know my little brother better and start over, yeah?"

Dee cocked an eyebrow at me. "And you're okay with this?"

I grinned. "Why not? He's like a lost puppy.

Can't just leave him out on the street. He also wouldn't stop following me... but, hey. Help's help. Say Ern, why don't you go get us some Joe?"

He gave a lazy salute. "You got it, Boss, no problem."

Dee watched him walk out and cross the street in disbelief. "You're enjoying this, aren't you?" she asked.

"Like you wouldn't believe," I chuckled, throwing a hand to the new desk. "Well. You got what you wanted. That one's yours, miss secretary."

A smirk rolled over her ruby lips, perching on the corner and running her hand along the smooth, lacquered surface. "I like it."

"Good to hear, doll." I took out a smoke and flicked on the lighter. "Good to hear. Now, get your pretty rear to work and get ready to take some notes. We have a client coming in for a case on a pretty sticky domestic dispute." I winked. "Which happens to be my new specialty."

**End**

# ABOUT THE AUTHOR

**Ellie** was born in Norcross, GA and raised by parents with a tremendous collection of books. While the shelves were predominantly stacked with science fiction and fantasy, they had several paranormal, noir, thriller, horror, and romance novels wedged in there, so she had a range to be influenced by. She currently still resides in Georgia with her loving husband and their keyboard-sitting cat.
Her site is: http://www.ellieraine.com/

Made in the USA
Columbia, SC
02 October 2018